Wild Indians
& Other Creatures
∎ ∎ ∎

Western Literature Series

Wild Indians
& Other Creatures

■ ■ ■

ADRIAN C. LOUIS

University of Nevada Press
Reno   Las Vegas   London

WESTERN LITERATURE SERIES

A list of books in the series appears at the end of this volume.

Some of these pieces have been published previously, sometimes in earlier versions, in *Aboriginal Voices, TriQuarterly, New Letters, The Lakota Times, Weber Studies, Ignis Fatuus Review, Blue Mesa Review,* and *The Chiron Review.* "Waylon Two Stars Takes His Son Rabbit Hunting" first appeared in *Among the Dog Eaters* by Adrian C. Louis (Albuquerque: West End Press). Copyright © 1992 by Adrian C. Louis. "The Blood Thirst of Verdell Ten Bears" was first published in *Blood Thirsty Savages* by Adrian C. Louis (St. Louis: Time Being Books). Copyright © 1994 by Time Being Press, Inc. Reprinted with permission. The epigraph by Thomas Merton is from *The Seven Storey Mountain* by Thomas Merton (New York: Harcourt Brace and Company). Copyright © 1948 by Harcourt Brace and Company.

www.unpress.nevada.edu

University of Nevada Press, Reno, Nevada 89557 USA
Copyright © 1984, 1992, 1994, 1995, 1996 by Adrian C. Louis
All rights reserved
Cover design by Erin Kirk New
Printed in the United States of America

The Library of Congress has catalogued the hardcover edition as follows:
Louis, Adrian C.
Wild Indians & other creatures / Adrian C. Louis.
p. cm. — (Western literature series)
ISBN 9780-87417-279-9 (hardcover : alk. paper)
1. Indians of North America—South Dakota—Social life and customs—
Fiction.
2. Pine Ridge Indian Reservation (S.D.)—Social life and customs—
Fiction.
I. Title. II. Series.
PS3562.082W5 1996 95-47239
CIP

The paper used in this book meets the requirements of American National Standard for Information Sciences—Permanence of Paper for Printed Library Materials, ANSI Z39.48-1984. Binding materials were selected for strength and durability.

Paperback edition published in 1997
ISBN 9780-87417-303-1 (pbk.)

This book has been reproduced as a digital reprint.

For Colleen with all my love.
For those who taught me and
for those I taught.
And for those red wetbrains
who refuse to come in
out of the rain.

*Therefore all the things around you will be
armed against you, to deny you, to hurt you,
to give you pain, and therefore to reduce you to solitude.*

*And when you have been praised a little and loved a little I
will take away all your gifts and all your love and all your
praise and you will be utterly forgotten and abandoned and
you will be nothing, a dead thing, a rejection. And in that day
you shall begin to possess the solitude you have so long desired. And your solitude will bear immense fruit in the souls
of men you will never see on earth.*

—*Thomas Merton,* The Seven Storey Mountain

Contents

How Coyote Got Killed
and Resurrected

High Plains. The last Thursday of March. Brilliant sunshine at eight in the morning. The unseasonable fifty-five-degree temperature made Coyote feel slightly sexual. And he had woke up with the remnants of a dream in which he was in bed with a strange woman. The warmth of the dream lingered with him, probably because his wife had been gone all month visiting relatives in California.

He raised his lean frame onto his hind legs, put on a windbreaker, and went out to rake the yard where snowdrifts had melted. After a half hour, he had a huge collection of dead leaves, cigarette butts, dog poop, and bleached-out beef bones. Beads of sweat popped off his snout. Clean, non-alcoholic sweat. For four years running, there had been no beer cans or wine bottles in his yard. Four years since the day he quit the sauce, the day he began to see daylight at the end of the slimy tunnel that had been his life. It had been almost two years

1

since he and his mate, Wanda, left the reservation and moved twelve miles south across the state line to Heinzville, Nebraska.

This cowturd town of twelve hundred souls was roughly one-third Indian and two-thirds White. Of those White two-thirds, one-third had an Indian in-law somewhere and the remaining third were just corpulent, cow-copulating rednecks.

Bending down to scoop the pile into a square-point shovel, Coyote saw the town dogcatchers setting a wire trap across the street in a corner of the elementary school playground. The two cowboy-clad women were redneck-decked from Stetsons to dung-heeled Tony Lamas.

Young, tall, lean, and sinewy, they sneered at Coyote as he continued to scrape up the dog poop. His first thought was what it would take to make them tumble to the dust in a fight. He strategized. Maybe bite one on the butt and grab her partner's ear and rip it off. Then go to work on them with his claws while they're howling. Coyote began to drool at the thought of wrestling the two female dogcatchers.

They were laughing to each other when Coyote saw one take a small bottle of liquid and dab a few drops inside the cage. Coyote pondered. Maybe it was some sex scent that made free-roaming dogs want to enter the cage. Maybe it was imitation sirloin perfume. More likely, it was the distilled souls of the dogcatchers themselves, he decided.

Here they were, on land stolen from the Indians, and yet these humans continued to torment Indians and dogs. The only dogs in the dog pound were wild Indian dogs. But these two city employees were fine-looking White women, and no doubt many Indian dogs drooled at the prospect of being caught by these dogcatchers.

When the dogcatchers caught the stray dog of a White citizen, they called the citizen up and asked him to please come get his dog. With Indian dogs, it was a twenty-five-dollar fine, and the fine increased with any backtalk or show of hostility by either the dog or its master.

The sheriff's department had a similar policy with humans. In the park last year, the nephew of the district judge clubbed some Indian winos in the head and rolled them. He got away with it. In Borden, another cowturd town eleven miles east, a cop shot an Indian in the back the year before and got away with it. And cattle ranchers were always shooting innocent coyotes that had meandered out past the city limits. Of course, it went without saying that they too got away with it.

That's just how things were. That's why Coyote looked at the dogcatchers as opponents in a cosmic struggle of good versus evil, or maybe madness versus sanity. Last year the same dogcatchers captured Gizzard, his Pekinese attack dog, for no reason. Because of such lunacy, Coyote thought the whole White world was deranged. And wherever he went, he always had their faint odor of insanity clinging to his hide. That was because whenever Coyote encountered lunacy, he wrestled it to the ground. Bits of craziness clung to him like cowpies hugging the sneakers of jogging hayseeds. That's just how things were.

Coyote had gone down to the sheriff's office and demanded the release of Gizzard hours after they took him. The dogcatchers weren't under their command, the sheriff's deputies smugly told him.

"Well, then, who?" Coyote asked, feigning anger. He could not control his desire for the dogcatchers.

"The mayor," they said. "And besides," they added, "them girls was only following orders, for Christ's sake."

Stunned by their arrogant stupidity, Coyote could only think of the ongoing massacre of his own fine-furred race. And dogs, well, dogs were his first cousins. Eventually, though, he had gotten his Pekinese freed. And as one of the dogcatchers handed his dog back, she had made a point of staring point-blank at Coyote's groin.

Now they were messing with him again. And he was excited again. When the dogcatchers were done setting their trap, they cruised off in a battered GMC pickup with a faded city decal. Three times in the next ten minutes, they circled his block. On their third pass, Coyote hopped his white picket fence and got out to stop their truck.

Every night his old lady, Wanda, jogged past where they'd put that trap, he told them. They remained impassive.

"My old lady gets caught in there, I'm gonna come looking for you, both of you illiterate yahoos. I know where you babes live," he said.

"Well, by all means, please do come on by," one said.

"*Parlez vous ménage à trois?*" said the other.

They glanced at each other with raised eyebrows, smiled, and then drove off, peeling rubber. Five minutes later, two sheriff's squad cars screeched to a stop in front of his yard. Four cops grabbed Coyote and threw him to the ground.

His face was pressed against the pile of dog poop and bones. He didn't move, thinking of Rodney King and knowing firsthand what a police baton felt like when it kissed the fur. They cuffed him and dragged him to a squad car. Then they hauled him to the county jail and charged him with threatening two peace officers. The dogcatchers had caught an angry Coyote this time.

Coyote was placed in a small cell at the end of a short hallway. The female jailer could monitor him in a round mirror suspended outside his cell. The jailer was hefty, flame-haired, and she had big milk-cow eyes that fluttered behind some archaic, black-framed glasses. She had Coyote locked in a staredown.

Coyote flopped on the metal cot, spat at the wall, and gently caressed his private parts, wondering if she might get off watching him do that. He thought of the two dogcatchers and his groin began to grow. In an instant, his shiny red tallywhacker was out and he was ready to squirt. He spasmed, saw stars, and howled at the top of his lungs: "Arrrroooooo!" His action was done more out of contempt than sexuality. He was disgusted with the entire system.

"Now, let's have a cigarette, *liebchen*," he said as he zipped up his pants and stared straight into her glutinous eyeballs.

The bulky Teutonic jailer walked up to his cell and smiled. She blew him a kiss and then shot him squarely in the heart with a .357 Magnum. Coyote ricocheted off the walls and then crumpled into bloody stillness. He was dead, stiff as a board when hours later a city janitor tossed him in the back of the pickup and drove him to the boondocks, where he quite unceremoniously dumped Coyote's carcass.

Three days later, on Easter Sunday, Old Bear went looking for a cigarette to borrow and stumbled upon a pile of fur and bones stinking up the High Plains sand. He looked closely and saw it was his old friend Coyote.

"Yo, Cootie Coyote, dude, are you dead or just trying to fake me out?" Old Bear asked.

"For sure I'm dead, ayyy," Coyote said in a barely audible whisper. "Whaddya think, I'm down here doing aerobics or maybe discussing Nietzsche with the grains of sand?"

"Got a cigarette I can borrow?" Old Bear asked as he took off his seed cap and wiped the sweat from the inside band.

"That nasty crud is what killed me. That and a bullet from a *federale's* .357 Magnum," Coyote said and then laughed and pointed his finger at his friend. "If you don't quit smoking, Bear, then you'll be a dead bag of bones too."

"Awww," Old Bear said and scooped up what was left of Coyote in his arms and carried him back to his cave. He sat Coyote down in an easy chair and offered him some leftover watermelon soup.

"Watermelon soup? Yuck and yuckity," said Coyote.

"Well, howzabout some hot macaroni casserole? I'll make it the way Unci taught me. First you boil the macaroni, then put it in a casserole dish and add a can of tomatoes, chopped-up onion, and some shredded commodity cheese. Then you cover it with bread crumbs and bake it good. We gotta put some meat on your bones. Make you able to get a moon-howling boner again."

"What for?" Coyote asked. "I'm dead. Deader than a doornail. Deader than a dinosaur fossil. Deader than a Mother Superior's cobwebbed bloomers. I'm old and dead and what's worse, I got some bad news for you, my friend."

"So lay it on me," Old Bear said and went about making his casserole anyway.

"You're dead too, you simple bugmugger!"

"Ayyyyyy. Always the trickster . . ."

"Look in the mirror, Bear," Coyote laughed. "Look into your eyes. You'll see you're no longer there. Go ahead. Go look. I ain't bullshellacking you. I mean, look at what's going on. We'd have to be in some nether world for us to even communicate."

"You're so full of crap," Old Bear said. "We've been friends for years. And you've been a bullshitter as long as I can remember."

Nevertheless, Old Bear walked to the bathroom and stared at his eyes in the mirror. He winked and blinked and stared again. Sure enough. Coyote was right. He was not inside his eyes. He splashed some cold water on his face and looked again. He was not inside his eyes. Maybe he was as dead as Coyote. He walked back to the kitchen, where Coyote was up and messing with the casserole, pouring Tabasco sauce all over it. Coyote winked.

"You always had a thing for Mexican food," Old Bear said and put the casserole back in the oven.

"Well?" Coyote said.

"Well, what?"

"Tell me whatcha seen," Coyote laughed. "It ain't the end of the world. Being dead ain't *that* bad, my man. Ninety percent of these humans walking around are dead and don't know it. For reals!"

"No more bedroom Olympics, no more hide-the-salami," said Old Bear and then sat down on his haunches and began to bawl.

"Yo, Bear. You ain't had none in more than ten years anyways. So what are you crying about?"

"At least I could fantasize and choke the chicken," said Old Bear as he reached for a Kleenex.

"Don't do no good to fantasize," said Coyote. "It was my lust for them dogcatchers that got me into trouble in the first place. But if it'll make you feel better, we can add a can of tuna fish to the casserole."

"*Ennut!*" said Old Bear. "Now you're talking. Here, give me your hide and I'll get you straightened out."

Coyote handed him his hide and Old Bear put it in his washer, then his dryer, and finally he ironed the old fur.

"Try this on for size," he told his old friend. Coyote put his hide on and didn't look half bad, almost spiffy. Bear brushed his own hair and splashed some Aqua Velva on his hairy face. He handed the bottle of aftershave to his buddy. Coyote gargled with it and then swallowed the turquoise liquid.

"We're going to tell each other that we are alive, and if we say so, we must be. To prove it, we're going out," Old Bear said and winked slyly. "Yessiree, we're outta here."

"Out where?" Coyote asked.

"I know a couple old blonde English teachers who work over at the Indian school. They always looked dead to me and besides, it's a holiday. They ain't working. We're gonna go see if they can still huff and puff and kiss fur good."

"I sure hope you got some conundrums," Coyote said.

"Always," said Old Bear. "That's all I'd need now is to catch me some of that human plague virus. End up wired to tubes and machines, babbling death songs and looking like a skeleton."

"No shit, Sherlock, I'm with you on that, even if we are possibly dead anyways," Coyote said as he and his friend diddlybopped out of the cave and across the chilled sands toward the Indian school.

"Human nooky ain't half bad in a pinch," Old Bear said.

"It's okay, I guess, but it's nothing compared to a badger or a skunk. And ooo-la-la, man, them funky skunks can get you going," Coyote said and made a gesture pinching his nose. Coyote never mentioned sex with female coyotes in front of Old Bear, and Old Bear never discussed sex with female bears in front of Coyote.

"I sure could use a cigarette," Old Bear said.

"Me too, brother," Coyote answered. They were walking in a sweet blue haze. The early spring sun was limp and refused to evaporate the Aqua Velva that they reeked of.

"My casserole!" Old Bear screamed suddenly. "I left the damn oven on. It'll burn down my cave."

"Geez-Louise, are you getting Alzheimer's or what?" Coyote asked.

"I really gotta go back," Old Bear said and turned.

"Sheeeeez," Coyote said and fell to the sand, a heap of fur and stinking bones.

"Sorry," Old Bear said. "Rest your bones just a while."

"Just let me be dead in peace," Coyote whined.

"Don't be so dramatic, just give me twenty minutes," Old Bear laughed. "Then I'll be back and we'll both get us a piece."

Old Bear got back to his cave, and the air was thick with the delicious smell of casserole. He couldn't resist it. He ate the whole thing and then fell asleep. He dreamed a dream so wondrous, so fantastic and beautiful that it does not bear repeating because no humans except a few old-time Indians would ever understand it. It was a dream of green beauty and flowers when humans and animals were the best of friends.

Then he awoke and went to help his dead friend Coyote get laid. And they did. And it was okay. Not great, just okay. Coyote went home and finished the yard-raking he had started a few days earlier. The very same dogcatchers were cruising their city truck around his block. Coyote went inside and closed the blinds on all his windows. He peeked out at them and when he was sure they were gone, he went back outside and continued raking. Those White girls sure were pretty. Pretty and pretty damn dangerous.

Why Coyote
Knotted His Whanger

Five months later, toward the end of summer, Coyote heard a noise and peered up over the sagebrush where he had been snoozing in the wilting heat ever since Wanda kicked him out of the house for flirting with the dogcatchers. He saw the last cowboy and the last cowboy was not on television or on the silver screen.

The last cowboy looked like he could have been a clone of Ross Perot, but he had a red neck and was clearly a dried-out drunk. He was standing on a deserted highway winding wearily through the Nebraska sandhills. The oven of late summer was cooking the last cowboy's stringy flesh. His car had broken down and he had no cash to fix it. He was broke, too broke to even pay attention.

The last cowboy looked around and swore up a storm. No houses, telephones, or televisions were in sight. Coyote could almost hear the cowboy doing an assessment of his sad life.

He was middle-aged, broke and jobless, with two heart attacks and one gall bladder job in the body bank, and his wife was unabashedly boinking a younger man.

Coyote suspected that invisible electric vultures were circling the old shitkicker's brain, waiting for the last gasp of common sense, for the last tango of his tough, white meat.

"Howdy there, Mr. Hopalong," Coyote yelled at the human and he rose to his hind legs and waved.

"Hummmmppphhh," the last cowboy answered.

Coyote reached into his cooler, grabbed an icy bottle of Budweiser, and walked upright toward the old cowboy.

"Thirsty?" Coyote asked.

"Faaaaact. That's a fact. Thirsty and angry," the old man said and reached for the beer.

"Well, you're thirsty and angry. I'm sad and horny as hell and living in the bushes to boot," Coyote said and winked.

"Christ, I hope you ain't one of them perverts," the man said.

"No, I'm hetero," Coyote said and flexed his bicep.

"Hetero? What's that?"

"I'm a straight arrow. I ain't no pervert. So what's the matter with your ride? Outta gas or what?"

"Broke down. Life shouldn't be this hard for a White man who's been to war but never to jail."

"I was just released from the can five months ago," Coyote told him. "Was charged with assaulting some dogcatchers verbally, but then the jailer killed me."

"Never heard such crapola," the old cowboy said. "But you never can tell these days. The whole country's going to hell in a handbasket. When they took God out of the classroom, they took God out of America."

"Hmmm," Coyote murmured and scratched at some fleas dancing around his groin. "And which God might that be?"

"The only one, god damn it," said the cowboy as he squinted

suspiciously at Coyote. "The Lord God of the Bible. Yahweh."

"My way, Yahweh, whatever," said Coyote as he heard something and perked his ears up. He turned his head quickly and saw a spiraling dust cloud in the distance. When it approached, he was able to see it was nothing but a brown UPS truck speeding across the land.

"And the Darkness is creeping from south to north. Here, even here in the Heartland the Darkness is corrupting, threatening and changing, scaring and scarring," the old man said and took a long drink.

"Hmmm," Coyote said. "Darkness, huh?"

"My own teenaged kids done quit school and now dress like those dirtbag gangster rappers on MTV," the cowboy said. "But legislation demands my tolerance. It's against the law to openly oppose the Darkness. I feel so helpless. What the holy hell happened to my country?"

Coyote spit and shrugged.

The old cowboy restarted his flapping jaws. "It wasn't so bad when it was only them Indians we had to put up with. It wasn't so bad when it was only them lazy good-for-nothing Prairie Niggers."

In the distant sky Coyote saw an eagle soaring.

"Look," he told the last cowboy. "An eagle. A good omen."

The old cowboy craned his neck skyward. Coyote let out a deep sigh and then another. He regretted that his civic sense had led to this. Coyote snatched back his bottle of beer and ran off into the shimmering heat. Coyote had once been married to an Indian girl. And he didn't like people bad-mouthing his ex in-laws.

"Up yours, you race cyst," Coyote yelled, thinking the old man was out of hearing range.

"Yeah, you'd like to, wouldn't you, you damned hairy pervert," the last cowboy gasped and flipped his middle finger into the air.

"Maybe. Bend over and we'll both find out," Coyote hooted, not wanting the old White man to have the last word.

Two weeks later, Coyote was back in the slammer. Smoking a cigarette, on his back on his jail cot, Coyote had weird visions of his dogs marching outside the county jail carrying signs. He'd been in cold storage a week this time. He'd actually been charged with stealing beer from the old White cowboy! The old man had gone down to the sheriff's department and filed charges against him. Unreal! So much for good deeds.

The day after he was arrested, the *federales* offered to let him go with a simple twenty-five-dollar fine for disturbing the peace, but he told the sheriff to go doublejointed upon himself. The sheriff turned red, said the hell with you, and tried to grab Coyote through the cell bars, so Coyote hocked a big green loogie on him.

"You want to die again, just keep that up," the sheriff said.

"I'm a political prisoner," Coyote said lamely, not that he had that much fear of death anymore.

The next day they hauled Coyote before the magistrate and gave him seventeen days in jail, minus time served. The original business with the dogcatchers was discussed. He told the judge he didn't want the local *gendarmes* to mess with any dogs because all dogs were his cousins. Leave them alone, he said, or he'd be before his bench again.

"Who's John Darms?" the judge asked and gave him a stern yet quizzical look. The judge had that dangerous combination of no education and no sense of humor. He was a forty-five-year-old white-haired man with a lifelong case of severe acne. He'd spent most of his life growing wheat.

"Never mind," Coyote said. "I just want my dogs left alone."

"I make the rules around here," the judge said.

"Rules rule," Coyote said and winked his mind's eye. The truth was that Coyote didn't want the dogcatchers to leave his dogs alone. He wanted them to mess with him. They were so pretty. And his shiny redness was getting firm.

Coyote wasn't always so protective of his cousins the dogs. He wasn't always so protective of himself either, or anyone he loved, for that matter. For nearly twenty years he had lived in the ethereal dusk of the bottle. His soul, his fears, his hopes and dreams were anesthetized daily, and of course, that's why people and animals too became addicted to alcohol. At least that's what it said in the AA booklet he had started to carry with him these days.

Coyote knew that the sauce obliterated reality. That much was obvious. It was also no big cosmic secret that fire water soothed fears. When he sobered up four years ago, Coyote came to know the beauty of dogs as he had during his childhood. He began to communicate with them, and they became partners in his new, sober world. They became his main companions, much to the chagrin of his old lady, Wanda. Wanda had never really liked dogs much after one slipped her his bone when she was in her teens. It had been a Great Dane.

"I don't see why you like them or even why they like you still," Wanda said one day. "You used to bite them and really treat them nasty when you were still drinking. Make them go without food for days."

True. Yes, he did. But these dogs he had now had never been abused by him. He got them after he sobered up. What she meant was that he had abused his other dogs, Pee Bear and Puppy Luppy. Worse, he was responsible for their deaths. That had happened five years earlier, in the final year of his seemingly eternal binge. Pee Bear was an English retriever. He showed up in Coyote's yard as a puppy, a brown, round ball of love who resembled a teddy bear. But he was untrainable inside and peed constantly on the rugs, so Coyote named him Pee Bear.

Puppy Luppy was a black Lab he found under the stairs of the tribal college center in Manderson. He, too, was a young puppy when Coyote brought him home. He named him Puppy Luppy and then shortened that to Lupper. They were tough-guy Rez dogs when they matured two years later. They kept winos and thieves away from his house and kicked tail on any stray dogs who came down his dirt road.

The two dogs had a wild-ass streak and chased cattle and once killed a young heifer, which Coyote then loaded up in the back of his small station wagon and took home and butchered. They feasted for a week on steaks, ribs, and succulent roasts. Later that month, Coyote took them hunting again and a rancher shot the dogs dead.

Remembering the fine, tender, grease-dripping meat made Coyote drowsy. He fell back to sleep and dreamed of the pan-fried liver and onions he would ask his wife to cook for him once he got out of the slammer. Sweet onions, batter-dipped, golden liver, and freedom. He slept and salivated and woke up hungry and remembered that Wanda had indeed kicked him out of the house.

For a moment he was unsure whether he was still dreaming or not. The fire-haired jailer was standing outside his cell. Her chunky flesh was vibrating, and Coyote could smell her excited sex, but he forced himself to ignore her. He'd read the recent papers about that woman in Virginia who'd chopped off her husband's wiener. Besides, he'd learned his lesson. He'd *learned* his lesson. His whanger wasn't going to get him into trouble again. He reached down underneath the thin jailhouse blanket that was covering him and tied it into a knot. He didn't know whether it felt good or bad, but he knew it felt safe.

He smiled, closed his eyes, and pretended to sleep until the mean fire-haired woman walked away. He didn't want to be killed twice in the same lifetime by the same woman. Such lunacy was possible.

Raven in the Eye of the Storm

Raven and his Sioux wife, Alicia, watched the storm building all day long. The thick white thunderheads towered and formed evil smiles on their blank but deadly faces. That fit the mood of Raven's life. Everything in the Raven household was disintegrating. The day before, their washer had stopped in midcycle and their telephone service had been shut off. Then their three poodles had peed on the rug after running in the yard all morning. The cigarette-scarred dining room table stood on two legs, levitated by the pile of unpaid bills at one end.

Under the slate sky early in the afternoon, the lawnmower had thrown a rod during his brown-skinned wife's five-minute turn and Raven sensed a conspiracy. A conspiracy of *Alicia's*. She was to blame for every starving child in Somalia. Even though she had a model's body, she was to blame for the angry boil on Raven's bony thigh. Even though she was kind and had the most beautiful face in the county, she was to blame for his anger. Raven's tongue turned purple because he had tied it in knots to garrote the procession of angry words. He could not do the same with his thoughts. They ran rampant:

She's got to be the most incompetent woman in the world. Why are the good-looking ones always the most helpless?

Just once when I'm weak I wish she'd come to me and say, "Okay, I'm taking charge of this expedition and I'm gonna fix all that's wrong. You just sit down and relax and watch some television. I'm gonna take care of you." Really!

This is all any American man or bird really wants to hear. Jesus, why can't women sense that men just want to be mothered?

And it wasn't just that the mower had quit on her turn. She didn't know how to work, period. When he went around the edges of the yard and made a square so that when her turn came she would only have to follow the tracks, she screwed up. She broke free of the established pattern and then got lost, wasting energy going over the same spots again and again. She had done the same thing when they'd painted their house.

Raven would cut in a square area for her to work and she would break out of it and make a mess, leaving holidays all over the place. Raven loved hard work efficiently done. He had done all kinds of human jobs and he had always been a hard, efficient worker. He had worked in the hay fields, in the copper mines, in the slaughterhouses. He had always done work the way it should be done, without the slightest hint of slacking off or taking the easy way out.

And he liked the concept of squaring work. He believed the entire known universe could be tamed by squares. Alicia had told him that Black Elk had said that White men had a skewed vision of life because they lived in square houses.

"Sometimes you think like a *wasicu*," she'd told him once when she still had the dregs of boldness, of innocent individuality in her.

"A black bird is about the farthest thing from a White man in the entire universe," he replied. "Besides, the *tipi* days are long gone. This is the twentieth century and work has to be done right, right?"

Raven didn't know if the philosophy of square houses was true or not, but he didn't believe what he'd read of Black Elk anyways. He viewed the old Indian subject of books by White men as little more than a sellout. Black Elk would probably have jizz-jinxed the lawnmower too, had the old coot been alive and not busy out peddling the sacred secrets of his people.

But Raven calmed those thoughts inside his brain and then stormed away from the broken lawnmower. He quietly went inside to be calmed by the tubal glare of electronic genocide. A television was a perfectly shaped square. The constantly running mind-control machine was showing a rerun of *Doogie Howser,* the goofy-hormonal-genius-M.D. of goofy-hormonal-idiot-writers, but Raven didn't like his looks, so he switched to *Cuisine Rapide* with Pierre Franey. Pierre was cooking up a mess of ginger chicken–stuffed cabbage.

"Ah, Pierre, *mon frère,*" Raven cackled.

"Do you want something?" Alicia said from the kitchen, trying hard to appease him, trying hard to be the dutiful wife.

"Nothing that you can do," he said between clenched teeth.

He heard Alicia scurrying around like a mouse up in the bedroom, the nunnery she always retreated to. And he thought of how she'd been a Bride of Christ and how the Catholic Church deadened her brain, stole her soul, and made her truly unable to make decisions on her own.

Once, when she'd been drunk, she had revealed that when the other Brides of Christ discovered the golden rod of Jesus was iron pyrite, they sleepwalked the heavenly halls and awoke in their sisters' arms. In the early years of their marriage, Raven would get drunk and call her a bulldagger . . . and she would cry and stare daggers back at him. Sobered, he would apologize, truly mortified by his drunken actions.

"I don't know why you say that," she would say. "I never did anything with anybody until I married you."

"Well, you did me on our first date," Raven sneered.

"But we fell in love."

"How many guys have you told that to?"

"I swear I fell in love with you from the start," she whimpered.

"It's impossible to fall in love on the first date," Raven said, but beyond his scorn he knew what she said was true. He had fallen in love with her when he'd first seen her. What he could not fathom was how he had fallen out of love with her.

Raven sat watching the tube and thought of how he had intimidated her through the years. He was almost ready to apologize for getting pissed about the lawnmower when she came down and apologized because the lawnmower had exploded on her watch. Then Raven got angrier than he'd been in years because he could clearly see that it was her fear of him that made Alicia shoulder the failure of mechanics.

"God damn French weenie," he shouted at Pierre Franey. Alicia jumped when he shouted. This increased Raven's anger. He gave her his meanest glare and didn't answer when she asked twice more if there was anything she could do. There were so many more bad things he wanted to say to her, but he saw she was shaking and having a hard time forming words. He was shaking too, his heart beating faster than any fluttering bird heart should.

Raven turned his eyes back to *Cuisine Rapide* and the ginger chicken–stuffed cabbage. The chicken and herbs were processed into a paste and then spread over wilted cabbage leaves. The process was repeated until what emerged was a sort of sandwich, cabbage leaves substituting for bread. Then the whole organism was set inside a towel and somehow twisted into a little green ball. Twisting completed, the beast now resembled a grapefruit-size cabbage. It could be either baked or steamed, Pierre told his invisible audience. Then he patted the rounded balls until they became semi-squared. Even Pierre knew the concept of squaring work, it seemed.

"Pierre, which is best," Raven mumbled. "Should it be steamed or baked? Try the oven. The oven is square."

Pierre did both and then served the cabbage with some sort of delicious-looking red sauce. Raven had missed the part that named the sauce's ingredients, but dagnabbit, he wished he had some. All the while, his wife stood silent awaiting his answer. He knew he was as cruel as the collective consciousness of Serbia. *Great Spirit, help me,* he silently prayed and fought to keep a tear from forming in his left eye.

"I'm sorry," Alicia said for the umpteenth time.

The storm was erupting in the distance, so he tried to talk softly to his wife. It wasn't her fault, he told her. He stared at the ripe firmness of her breasts bulging against her black T-shirt. He tried to explain how everything was conspiring against them.

"It ain't *all* your fault," he said.

"It isn't?" By now Raven had convinced her that anything that went wrong was her fault.

"It isn't?"

"No, Alicia. I'm sorry. Sorry and starving."

She was so happy that she wasn't being blamed that when he said he was hungry she volunteered to run to the White man's store for cold cuts, pickles, cottage cheese, and Oreos. Anything he wanted.

Half an hour later, Raven was chomping factory-pressed and sliced chicken and cottage cheese and pretending he was at Pierre's house, slurping cabbage, when the cutting edge of the bad weather hit. The storm was a vicious beast and as uncaring as Raven sometimes was. Sheet lightning struck a van in his neighbor's yard and set it afire. Sixty-mile-per-hour winds swirled a fog pregnant with golfball-sized hail. It was typical High Plains madness. The elements danced their dangerous witchery.

In ten minutes there were hailstone drifts a foot deep. All the trees in his yard were stripped leafless and their zucchini and tomato garden was battered into a pulpy red and green sauce. Raven could not see an inch of lawn that was not covered with deep hail. He screamed at Alicia to take the three poodles down to the basement.

"What?" she said in a frightened voice.

"The dogs!" he bellowed.

"Do what?" she asked, puzzled by his cryptic directions.

"Cawwwwkkkk!" he yelled, so loud that for an instant the approaching storm was all but drowned out. "Damn, damn, damn. Can't you do anything right?" he shouted and hopped up into the air and flapped his wings at Alicia.

She went mute. His screaming had scared her so much that she stood there, paralyzed, unable to move or talk. He screamed again, but she still didn't move, so he called her a "dumb useless human bitch." She remained motionless.

"Alicia, get your head on straight! Get the dogs and get down into the basement. It might be a twister." He still got no response.

The upstairs windows blew out and shattered. Books air-danced from his shelves and he dodged them.

He jumped into the air, brought his beak to her nose, and shouted madly, "You're hopeless! Damn, you're hopeless!"

Alicia just stood there like some weird female zombie or maybe like a catatonic child. Raven's eyes began to bug out. He saw a trickle of saliva run down from the corner of his wife's mouth. Then a slight, crooked smile formed on her face.

"Holy Mary, Mother of God," she finally murmured.

Raven's own face was greener than Pierre's cabbage. His

brain spun out of his skull and ricocheted around the square room. For an instant, he thought he saw a faint halo around his wife's head. That was the last thing Raven saw before the vortex sucked him out the window and up into the sky of either hell or freedom. He didn't know which and he sure didn't care. But he was happy. He was happy that Alicia would finally be free of his tyranny. And vice versa.

He spun through the sky. The sky was as black as his feathers. The sky was as black as his sins. He wondered if they would have ginger chicken–stuffed cabbage in heaven. It didn't matter. He was sweating, trying to fly squares in the black sky. He was working the storm for all he was worth, which wasn't all that much.

Pretty Bull
Schemes a New Snag

When Timmy John Pretty Bull was clean and sober, he often admitted to himself that he was one very bright Indian. It was only when he was drinking that things went askew and he acted like a dumb-ass. He'd been drinking when he left the South Dakota plains and attended the large powwow in Minneapolis. He figured it was the drinking that had triggered his chest pains. Exactly what the stitcher at the emergency room there told him. He wasn't having a heart attack at all—Mr. Heart was fine.

"Stress and booze," the doctor said. "Stress and booze."

But, his heart wasn't fine at all six months later when a scumbag bill collector hired by the Minneapolis emergency room began calling his house day and night. This put him on edge and set him to drinking even harder. Then one morning, wonder of wonders, he woke up sober and the phone was ringing. It was the bill collector again.

"We're going to take legal action against you unless this bill is paid by the end of the week," the feminine-voiced man in Minneapolis said. Timmy John was distressed by this. He *had* gone up to the PHS Indian hospital and *had* tried to get them to cover the bill, which amounted to close to three hundred dollars for a twenty-minute visit. They had refused to pay it. In essence they said Timmy John wasn't covered by them once he left the reservation.

"You mean once I leave the Rez I ain't a Indian?" he scoffed at them, then stomped out the door and went off on another binge.

And so it led to the weak-voiced *wasicu* man harassing him. He said his name was Willard Wentworth. The collection firm's name was Allied Accounts Unlimited.

"Mr. Pretty Bull, we will have to take legal—"

"Only a vagina would got a job like yours," the sober Mr. Pretty Bull said and hung up. He liked the sound of that word. Vagina.

The phone continued to ring every five minutes for the rest of the day. Every time he picked it up, Timmy John said, "Vagina" and hung up. This made his wife, his mother-in-law, and several other people highly pissed off because they'd happened to call his house.

"How come you called me and Mom a vagina when we phoned here today?" his wife asked. "You drunk again or what?"

Timmy John looked at Velva, his two-hundred-pound wife, and apologized. Well, at least he tried.

"I thought it was that bill collector," he said sheepishly. "I know you ain't a vagina, I mean, uh, well, forget it." He had called Willard Wentworth of Allied Accounts Unlimited a vagina because Mr. Wentworth definitely sounded feminine. Now, Timmy John had nothing against men of the gay persuasion. In fact, one of his closest friends was Fat Louie, and everyone on the Rez knew that Fat Louie was a *winkte*.

What he had really meant was that no real man would ever have a job calling people to collect money. That form of nagging was best suited to women. And to Timmy John, men who acted like women were vaginas, regardless of whether or not they were homosexual. No man who had any *cojones* would stoop to such a demeaning, chickenshit job. And Timmy John knew this man could yank the strings of his Indian emotions at will from the anonymous bricks of Minneapolis.

And that night at midnight, the man yanked again.

"Mr. Pretty Bull, this is Willard Wentworth—"

"Willard of St. Paul. How's it hangin'?"

"Fine, now about this bill, Mr. Pretty Bull."

"You live in St. Paul, right?" Timmy John asked in the brightness of a strange clarity that seemed to come from outside his own mind.

"Yes, but what's that—"

"Vaginaville," Timmy John said and hung up. Then the clarity grew even brighter. An idea gave birth to itself in his brain. He called Minneapolis-area information and found that a W. Wentworth did live in St. Paul. Then he called his first cousin Vern Ed Two Knives, who lived in Minneapolis. Vern Ed owed him many favors, and Vern Ed was one serious redskin badass, with a dozen different tattoos, one for each time he'd been in jail or prison.

Timmy John was six-two and two hundred pounds, but he always felt like a midget next to his cousin. Vern Ed was six-six and always hovered around three hundred pounds. He always carried a gun and never drove a car. He owned a Harley-Davidson and roamed the city with others of the lunatic fringe who also owned Harleys.

"What the hell you want this time of night?" Vern Ed asked when Timmy John called him. "Damn, Cuz, your sundial broken or what?"

"Get your phone book and see if there's a Willard Wentworth and see if he's got a address."

"Say what?"

"Just do it. You owe me favors."

"Yeah, he's in here on Carnette Drive in St. Paul," Vern Ed grumbled about a minute later. "So what about him?"

"I want you to go knock on his door and punch that sissy boy hard and square on his *wasicu* nose."

"You're kidding me, *ennut*? Hey, you drinking or what?"

"Hey, Cuz, not only am I sober, but I'm addressing a envelope to you right now. That envelope has four twenty-dollar bills in it. That's all I can afford, but this guy's really been messing with my head bad. Will you do him for me?"

"I'm getting dressed now," Vern Ed said and laughed. "You just want me to hit him once. That's all? Hell, I'd do that for free."

"Yeah, man. Just punch him a good one on the nose, and, well, if you feel like it, you can kick him in his sissy *cojones*."

"Sounds good to me," Vern Ed said and chuckled.

"Yeah, somehow I thought you'd like this assignment," Timmy John said and let out a high-pitched giggle. "You can pretend you're on *Mission Impossible* or something."

"That ain't on TV no more," Vern Ed said and waited.

"Well, okay, you can be Matt Dillon on *Gunsmoke*."

"Damn, Timmy John. Is your tube in a time warp or what? Both those programs ain't been on the TV in *dona* years."

"Well, be Sylvester Stallion or someone," Timmy John said and hung the phone up. He shook his head and shrugged. His cousin Vern Ed had never been known for his brainpower.

But Timmy John knew he would sleep better that night than he had slept in months. He just wished he could see Mr. Willard Wentworth getting his lights punched out by one tough-ass Sioux Indian. He felt so good that his groin started to glow, but when he crawled back into bed, Velva was snoring and had her hair in curlers. She didn't look too appetizing, so he gripped his trout and wrestled with it until it was all slippery. Then he slid under the sheets and entered a soft dream world where all the women were young and beautiful and had spending cash.

Two days later Vern Ed called and said the job had been easy. "That guy started to bawl after I hit his nose," he said. "Just crying like a little baby, so I punted his nuts and said he better leave Indians alone or I'd be back."

"He was really crying?"

"Yeah, man. Wahhhh. Wahhhh, wah-wah."

Timmy John felt pleased, so pleased that he decided to stay on the wagon. Like he always told himself, when he was sober, he was one bright Indian. And everything seemed to go just fine and the days flew by like chickens with their heads chopped off. He was working again and Mr. Willard Wentworth had not called in three months now. Everything was just jim-dandy, except that Velva had quit giving him sexual relief. She said she wasn't getting anything in return.

Timmy John agreed. She was getting too fat to enjoy anyway. He didn't like losing his hands and other parts of himself in the folds of her fat. And so he schemed to get a new snag. A young one. And he had just the right one in mind. Janella Slow Horse, who worked at the tribal commodity food warehouse with him.

Janella was short and slightly chubby, but she had a face that sent Timmy John into drooling fits. It was, to him, the most beautiful face on the entire Rez. She had sparkling dark brown eyes, and she wore round gold-rimmed glasses. Her lips seemed naturally red, and he dreamed about kissing them again and again and again.

He wondered if it was normal for a man in his late thirties to dream about kissing girls. He figured it was okay because she was so outstanding. Her only defect was that she spoke with a slight lisp, but her difficulty with the letter S hardly mattered to him. If she was with him, she wouldn't have time to talk because he'd be kissing her so much.

Janella's father, Abraham, was a medicine man, a *wicasa wakan*, and an elk dreamer to boot. Timmy John's understanding of traditional Lakota religion was vague at best. But he did know about the power of dreams, and he would create a dream to help him win the winsome Janella.

On Monday morning of the next week, Timmy John was unstacking a pallet of USDA beef stew when Janella walked by and made a note on her clipboard. She was the assistant inventory clerk.

"Morning beautiful Janella," he said. "I mean beautiful morning Janella," he said when he saw her glare at him.

"Uh-huh," Janella said in a voice that made sure he knew she was semi-management and he was just a laborer.

"I had a dream about you," he said and dropped a carton of canned stew onto a hand truck.

"Dream . . ."

"Yeah, I had a dream about you. Kind of a strange dream. I don't know, maybe I shouldn't even be telling you."

"What wath it about?" He had her hooked now.

"Naw, forget it. Just a silly, but very weird dream."

"Tell me."

"I don't think so. It was just too incredible."

"Tell me, damn you."

"I got work to do now. I guess if you really want to know, I could meet you for a drink after work," he said and stood straight and tried to form his most pleasing smile. He ran his hand through his long black hair and pushed it back. He knew that he wasn't a bad-looking guy.

"A drink? I thought thomeone thaid you were married."

"Well, my wife Velva and me are thinking about getting separated."

"I got a boyfriend," she said. "Red Thimp-Thimp-Thimpthon in the road department at the BIA."

"You go out with Red Simpson? He's a *wasicu*. How come you go out with a White guy?"

"Hey," she lisped. "You ain't here to debate my perthonal life. Technically, I'm your thuperior. You don't want to tell me your thilly dream, then the hell with you."

"This dream was unbelievable. Don't you believe in dream power? Come on, just one drink with me. Meet me at the bar over in Heinzville. At the Long Branch. Seven-thirtyish."

"Theven what?"

"Make it seven, okay?"

"Okay, damn it. Theven o'clock."

Timmy John sat staring into the beautiful eyes of Janella Slow Horse. She was wearing tight Levi's and a black satin jacket.

"Well, tell me what wath your dream?" she asked and slowly stirred the Seven-and-Seven he had bought her. Her hair was braided.

"Janella, it was weird. We was in this bedroom. It was all pink, had pink walls too. You was wearing a pink nightgown and—"

"I think I gotta go," she said.

"No, wait. In this dream you was wearing a pink nightgown and I was on my knees in front of—"

"You're a thick thon of a bitch."

"No, I'm not sick. Wait, let me finish," Timmy John said desperately and signaled the bartender for another round. He put his mind in high gear and tried to take his dream in another direction. He had her here with him, and he didn't want to lose the awesome beauty of her company.

"You were praying," he went on. "I was on my knees and you were praying over me. A Christian prayer. You had your hands on my forehead and were trying to get the evil spirits to leave my body. You said some strong prayers and they did leave. And you know what? After you prayed for me, you started talking normal like everyone else."

"Thath your dream? Really I thpoke normal?"

"Well, there's more," he said and wiped a bead of sweat from his chin. "Then all of a sudden we're out in the woods. Up on this ridge covered with pine trees. Then something started coming towards us in the bushes. You got scared and we both started hoofing it away from that sound. It mighta been a bear, we couldn't see."

"What a crathy dream."

"Then we both backed up into this bush and fell over ass-backwards into a big hole in the ground. It was so deep that it was pitch-black on the bottom. You started to cry, so I lit a match. I put my arm around you and told you not to worry. Then I made a small fire and then built a small ladder out of some branches that were scattered around. We crawled out and then you told me you loved me."

Janella's eyes were wide and puzzled when Timmy John finished his dream-story.

"I don't know what that meanth," she said.

"Me neither," he said. "But that's the dream I had."

"Buy me another drink," she said. And he did. And half a dozen more to boot. And he spent twenty-three quarters playing Hank Williams for her on the jukebox. And late that night, Timmy John Pretty Bull found out that the walls in Janella's bedroom really were painted pink. And the few words she spoke sounded quite normal to him except when she told him she was quitting her job.

"Why?" he said as he kissed her all over her face. "I was just thinking here I'm going to really look forward to going to work now."

"I'm getting a new one," Janella said and smiled. "You're looking at the new independent represhentative for Allied Accounth Unlimited of Minneapolith."

Badger Medicine
and Velva's Bloomers

Timmy John Pretty Bull hitched his jeans up and ran his hands through his long black hair. He breathed onto his glasses, found a clean spot on his T-shirt to wipe them, and then stared at Fat Louie LeBeau's turquoise HUD house. He blinked, winced, and knocked on the door. Fat Louie thought it was the Indian thing to do, so he had painted it with some discount paint called "Bright Albuquerque Blue." Because Fat Louie ignored his own perverseness, he could not hear his tribe snickering behind his back about the oddball paint job. Many said that only a *winkte* would paint his house that way. It only mattered sometimes to Timmy John that Fat Louie was gay because they had been friends off and on since childhood.

"*Entréz,*" Fat Louie shouted.

Timmy John entered and stared at the inside walls, which were painted pink. He blinked his eyes and lowered his head.

He was in rough shape because of a killer hangover, and the overpowering smell of Louie's soup almost made him gag. Louie always had a pot of soup cooking. Once, a year earlier, Timmy John had visited and Louie had offered egg salad sandwiches for lunch. Pretty Bull, hungover then too, had been startled to see Louie drop the eggs into his ever-cooking soup and boil them that way.

Now, like then, Timmy John's middle-aged mouth felt like it was full of used cottonballs and if he didn't keep a tight rein on his eyeballs, they manufactured visions of lizards running up his ankles. And then he had to deal with Fat Louie.

Sometimes he didn't like the idea of being in Fat Louie's house. Fat Louie was queer as a three-dollar bill, and though he'd never tried anything with Timmy John, Fat Louie still made him nervous, especially when he was sober and thought about it. He glanced at Louie and winced as he thought he caught a glimpse of a pink bra beneath his greasy mechanic's coveralls. On his skinniest day, Louie tipped the scales at three hundred pounds. His sparse hair looked like it had been dyed black. It was coal black, almost a blue-black, too black for even a fullblood.

Timmy John sat on the couch and watched Louie watching Phil Donahue interview some fat male cross-dressers. A gracious host, Louie had given him a cup of coffee with a saucer under it because he could see he had the shakes, but Timmy John was slopping coffee on the couch anyway. Louie didn't care. He was a mechanic and the couch had a good sheen of grease and oil on it already. Coffee probably wouldn't even penetrate the once-pink material.

"Well," Timmy John said and bounced the clattering cup and saucer onto the cigarette-burned coffee table. A big can of WD-40, a flock of battered screwdrivers, and a pile of *Good Housekeeping* magazines covered the table.

"Well, what?" Louie asked and then pointed with his lips at a fat man in wig, lipstick, miniskirt, and nylons on the tube.

"I *was* on the wagon again," Timmy John said.

"Yeah, but you always fall," Louie countered.

Timmy John reached for his coffee. "This time I fell off because Janella Slow Horse don't want to go out with me no more. She said it's too much trouble to be with a married man. And then her new job being a bill collector. I always got a good reason every time I fall. The time before when I fell off it was that doctor who drove me to drink. Goofy comedian Jew guy from New York out here saving us Skins from ourselves. Said to me sure go ahead and eat greasy food. Yeah, this doctor said that and then he laughed and said drink all you want. Can you believe it?"

"That don't sound like no doctor," Louie said and lit a cigarette.

"Yeah, he told me go ahead and take drugs to torque me up, down, or sideways. I knew he was doing reverse psychology or some kinda horseshit, so I asked would it be okay to screw sheep. Diddle badgers if you want, this doctor said, and then he tried to look tough. This doctor was a damn comedian."

"Badgers, huh?"

"No man alive never screwed no stinking badger. *Ennut*, only a city man would say something so ignorant like that."

"*Ennut*," Louie agreed. "Pure crazy."

"I think it was that badger business that set my brain on fire and made me fall off the wagon," Timmy John said. "Bad badger medicine."

"Say what?" Louie said and rolled his eyes.

"It's true, Louie!"

"Hey, man, I ain't got no time for no wino fantasies." Louie fastened his two small raisin eyes on Timmy John.

Timmy John averted his eyes and squirmed. Then he took a sip of coffee and smacked his lips, trying to show appreciation. "Two weeks later I was on a binge in Milan's Club down in Gallup, New Mexico, and this drunk Navajo says me a Navajo joke. He said: '*If you're not a Yazzie you must Begay.*'"

"What's that to do with badgers?" Louie asked, still staring hard.

"Well, everything's related in the sacred circle."

"Snot on a Ritz cracker," Fat Louie chortled. "Next thing you know, you'll be telling me to walk in balance on the good, red road."

Timmy John didn't really know much about badger medicine. In fact, the only time he had ever heard it mentioned was by a *wasicu* in the bank in Martin. He'd gone there to cash his wife's welfare check, and he'd overheard the president of the bank talking to a White customer. He was describing a beaded badger skin on the wall.

That poor, dead badger had its eyes sewn shut, and strange beadwork covered its stomach. The banker told the customer that the Sioux Indians believed the badger had strong medicine. Timmy John had glanced at the huge stack of twenty-dollar bills the customer was getting and his mouth drooled. *You can say that again*! That was about all he'd ever heard about badgers, but then he really wasn't into traditional Indian religion. Or any religion, for that matter.

"If you're not a Yazzie, you must Begay," Timmy John repeated.

"That don't make no sense to me," Louie said and tossed his pack of cigarettes toward his visitor.

"It's a Navajo joke," Timmy John said.

"They got a constipated sense of humor, then," Louie said.

Timmy John took one of the smokes, lit it, and said, "I didn't get it neither, but I laughed a little and that was my mistake. That Navajo saw an opening and tried to sell me this here turquoise ring." He flashed the ring at Louie, but Louie was still mesmerized by the White men on the tube who got off dressing up like women.

"They say they ain't homosexuals," Louie said and glanced at his visitor, who was still waving his ringed finger in the air.

"*Ya ta hey*," Timmy John squeaked. "Heyyyy, the silver on this ring ain't tarnished by either booze or werewolf blood. That damn sheephumper down there smiled at me, and his wolfy teeth were white as bleached bones."

"I wonder if them morfadykes make their wives dress up like men and get on top," Louie wondered aloud and pointed with his lips.

"I don't know," Timmy John answered. He wanted to swing the conversation back to the ring. *Morfadykes?*

"I wonder if they have their wives strap on dildos," Louie pondered, salivated, and squinted. His hand moved toward his groin.

"I don't know about that, but I do know that you don't see many drunks with such good teeth like that Navajo had," Timmy John said, eyeballing Louie. He took off the ring and rolled it from hand to hand.

"What is all this nonsense?" Louie lisped as the program ended. "Just what is all this silly crap, *tahansi*? Badgers, Navajos, rings? Damn, Cuz, I was really into that program."

"It's the ring," Timmy John said and chuckled nervously.

"It's just a ring. Big friggin' deal," Louie said and lit another cigarette. He put the pack in his pocket and didn't offer any more to Timmy John. Fat Louie was signaling that the visit was close to being over.

"To make a long story short, I bought the ring for twenty bucks. Couple weeks later I hitched back here to home base for treatment again. But, anyway, I'm drinking again. Givin' my liver aerobics. So listen, Cuz, what will *you* give me for this here turquoise ring? It's real, *ennut*, genuine Navajo. And it matches your house."

"No way, José," said Louie.

"Come on, *kola*, help me out. I'd do the same for you."

"Forget it. I ain't as dumb as I look."

"Please. I gotta get me some hair of the dog."

"Shit on a shingle," said Louie. "I buy that damn turquoise ring, I might as well buy me some women's panties and parade around on the *Phil Donahue* show."

"Ten bucks," said Timmy John.

"Two," said Louie. "Lemme see the damn ring. Probably won't even fit." He tried it on and it did. It fit him perfectly.

"Ten and I'll run over to my house and steal you a couple pair of my old lady Velva's bloomers," Timmy John said in desperation.

"Velva's bloomers?"

"Yeah, my wife's big, fat bloomers."

"Really? What color?" Louie asked, suddenly interested.

"What color you want?"

"If I got a choice then surprise me," Louie said.

"Then it's a deal?"

"Well, only 'cause you're my friend, Timmy John. It's a deal."

"Honest Injun?"

"Hey, there ain't no such thing," Fat Louie said with a grin.

"Well, here's the ring. Can I have that ten now? I'm really sick, really *kuja*. I got to get some medicine from Oren the Bootlegger."

"Grab some pink ones," he heard Louie shout at his back. "Some nice pink ones," Louie reiterated as Timmy John Pretty Bull left his house with a crumpled tenspot in his hand.

"Okay," Timmy John said low. "I'll get some nice fat, pink bloomers for you," he snickered. It was hard to get the words out past his huge and genuine grin. He hoped he could find some holey ones.

He had started at a brisk pace toward Oren the Bootlegger's when he saw something move in the wild cherry bushes lining the dirt road in front of Louie's house. For an instant, Timmy John thought it looked like a fat, low-riding badger. It might have been. It could have been, but he didn't care. He was headed for the house of cheap wine and nothing in the world would stand in his way.

Ten bucks! He'd only paid the Navajo five. And he was damned if he was going to give that pervert Louie his own wife's panties. He'd keep those for a hole card, money in the bank for a future dry day. He wasn't like the younger generation. At least once in a while he planned for the future. Not many people seemed to do that anymore. The whole world was going to hell in a handbasket. And these young kids, the boys were wearing pants way, way too large. So large that from the back it looked like they had dumped a load in their drawers. And they wore their caps backwards. Not to mention their strange sidewall haircuts.

When Timmy John was a kid, no one on the Rez collected welfare. Back then, people made do and took whatever kind of work was available. They hunted deer, grew gardens, and kept their yards neat. These days young boys knocked up girls and the Church blessed them and the government paid them. *Just look at my cousin Mariana*, he thought. The whole world was cockeyed and lopsided. Maybe the end of the world really *was* coming.

Timmy John slowed his trek and glanced back at Fat Louie's turquoise house. He looked at the money in his palsied left hand. Then he clearly saw a badger skittering down the street. No, he thought, *the end of the world is not coming. And today is going to be a good, good day, thanks to Mr. Badger and thanks to my wife Velva's bloomers.*

"Grandfather, thank you," he mumbled and stumbled away.

Sunshine Boy

When Mariana Two Knives was five years old, her grandmother told her an old story. Long ago, when the earth was very young and before the White man came to these shores, the animal and plant people were enjoying the beautiful summer weather. But as the days passed, the story went, autumn began to set in, and the weather became colder with each passing week.

The grass and the flower people were in sad shape because they had no protection from the bitter cold. Just when it looked like the end of the road, the Great Spirit came to their rescue. He told the trees to drop their leaves to form a warm blanket over the tender roots of the flowers and grass. To repay the trees for their kindness, he allowed them one last array of multicolored beauty.

"*Ennut,* Mariana. Just look outside and you'll see what I'm talking about," her grandmother would tell her. "What do you see, child?"

"Leaves all colors," Mariana said.

"Yes, all the pretty colors," her grandmother concurred. "A blanket for the mother earth in winter." That, her grandmother instructed, was why each year during Indian summer the trees donned their farewell robes of red, gold, and brown.

Mariana, who was now sixteen and good-looking in a rugged kind of way, recalled that old story as she sat drinking from a bottle of cheap Gibson's muscatel in an empty lot in the reservation village. She passed the quickly emptying bottle around with her drinking buddies.

"*Lila osni*," her best friend, Sandy, said. "It's getting pretty damn cold out here, *ennut*?"

"*Ennut*," Mariana agreed and reached awkwardly for what was left of the mind-bending liquid in the green pint bottle.

Winter was coming and soon she'd have to scheme to get some warmer clothes. The stupid trees wouldn't give her a blanket of leaves. And besides, she'd swallowed a watermelon seed. Damn these Indian men! Three months pregnant and her belly was beginning to rise noticeably.

"Hey, Roscoe," she said as a new wino joined the encounter group. "You got a short dog on you or what?"

"Yeah, you bet," Roscoe said and handed her a half-empty pint of white port. She took one, then another large gulp of the "Green Lizard" and shook her head and laughed.

She wasn't really sure who the father was. It could have been Charlie Boy Red Blanket, but then again, it could have been Verdell Ten Bears. Ten Bears was one handsome devil and she had been in and out of love with him since grade school. Then again, it could have been that damn Roscoe. He sure was ugly, but he always managed to come up with enough cash to score wine.

"You ain't gonna get lucky again tonight," she said to him as he sat next to her like a puppy dog. "You do look snitz though."

"You're gettin' a tummy on you," he said and handed her a pack of cigarettes. "You gotta take care of yourself, little sis," Roscoe teased.

"I ain't your damn sis," she spit and lit a cigarette. Yet it made her feel good that Roscoe did act just like a big brother. And, well, if he wanted to get her in the sack every so often, that was all part of the game. He was tolerable. He wasn't a bad guy, like so many of the useless drunks she hung out with. He was okay, but then the very next week he got ran over by some teenagers drag-racing their cars down Main Street. And Mariana had cried many tears when she'd found out about his death.

In the spring she gave birth to a chubby, dark boy. She named him Sherman, although she knew nobody with that name. It was a White man's name. The name fell off her lips awkwardly. Even as she named him, she knew that Sherman was a foolish name for an Indian, but she stuck with it. Her son was Sherman, for better or worse.

Sherman was severely retarded with a combination of Down's syndrome and fetal alcohol syndrome. He had a head like a pumpkin, a small brown pumpkin. There was little doubt that Mariana's drinking had contributed to his retardation. Retarded children were a quite common occurrence on the reservation. If Mariana had any guilt over the way Sherman looked, she did not speak of it. The baby boy, with his fish eyes, his cleft palate, and misshapen head, made his mother angry at the world, not at herself.

"I bet it was that damn Roscoe," she would mumble to her baby.

When Mariana got out of the PHS Indian hospital, she went to live with her auntie Angie, who was sixty and had diabetes. With her aunt's help, she quit drinking for two months but then went on a binge and stayed gone for four days. When she returned, her aunt had her old suitcase packed.

"You don't have no respect," Angie said. "Go and live with your wino friends if you want to drink all the time. Leave the boy with me. I can take care of him better than you."

"He's my baby," Mariana said with little fervor.

"He'll be here once you learn to be a mother," her aunt said.

Mariana was slightly humiliated but greatly relieved and felt like a great burden had been lifted from her. Though little more than a child herself, Mariana sensed that she wasn't fit for motherhood or much of anything except being a drinker, an outsider, maybe a bum. There was nothing she wanted to accomplish in her life. She really had no dreams.

"It's probably for the best," Mariana said and picked up her suitcase without even kissing Sherman good-bye.

"Kiss him before you go," her aunt demanded.

"Okay," Mariana said and gave Sherman a peck on the cheek.

"You think you can straighten out, then come home," Angie said and wiped at a tear forming in the corner of her eye. "Here, take this," she said and handed Mariana three twenty-dollar bills folded into a small triangle.

"Thanks," Mariana said and five hours later she had spent it all.

The seasons changed, and Angie watched over Sherman as if he were her own son while Mariana resumed her drinking ways and disappeared into the destructive fabric of the reservation.

When Sherman was two years old and his mother long gone, having left the reservation for the saloons and the back alley melodramas of Rapid City, he developed a profound love for the sun. For hours and hours each day, he would watch the sun floating on its bright journey from morning to evening. Though the sounds he formed made no sense to his aunt, she assumed he was singing songs of worship for the sun. His auntie Angie nicknamed him Sunshine Boy.

"*Wi*," she would whisper in Lakota and point at the sun and then tickle him. "*Wi, hoksila, Wi.*"

"*Wi*," Sherman would mimic and point at the sun too.

One hot summer day when Angie was busy watching her soap operas and Sherman was sitting in the backyard, tragedy struck. He had been staring directly at the sun for more than an hour, and he burned out some optic nerves. He was blinded by *Wi*, the one thing that he dearly loved besides his auntie Angie.

Angie was devastated and came very close to resuming drinking herself. The doctors up at the PHS hospital said he would never regain his vision. Angie had tried to get word to Mariana through some people she knew Mariana drank with, but her niece never came to see her own son.

"Damn that girl's hide," Angie would whisper and then cuddle Sherman and cry large, silent tears.

Sherman did not seem to mind or even notice his blindness. He still loved the sun and now would sit in the yard and follow the path of the sun by the heat of its rays on his face. All summer long he would swing his oddly shaped head at the unseen golden orb. He was happy and still sang his mumbling songs of honor, but in the fall he began to deteriorate physically. First he had a severe kidney infection, and then his kidneys failed. He was put on dialysis twice a week, a real hardship for a child his age. Soon he was confined to a wheelchair.

Angie would wheel him out into the backyard and set him facing the weak sun of early autumn. Sherman would smile and mumble "*Wi, Wi, Wi*" in a delighted whisper. Despite all his troubles, he could still smile. And then one day in mid-September, after he had been sitting in the sun for nearly an hour, his auntie Angie went to bring him inside for a sandwich and a glass of Kool-Aid.

"Time to come in, Sunshine," she sang to him. When he did not answer, she ran to him and screamed a mournful sound. Sherman was stiff, his mouth agape and almost smiling, and his blind eyes were wide open. The boy child was dead. Sunshine Boy had departed for the spirit world. The last spark of his life had left the prison of his body and had journeyed to the sun that he so dearly loved.

Sherman was buried in the Catholic cemetery at Holy Rosary Mission. It was a small funeral, attended only by a handful of Angie's AA friends, and Mariana was absent. No one knew where she was or how to find her. She had never shown the slightest love for Sherman anyway. Angie took care of all the funeral arrangements, even using most of her savings for a finely wrought casket that the local undertakers sold her, probably for three times what they'd paid for it.

When Sherman had been dead almost a year, Angie went up to the cemetery to lay some flowers on his grave and chop down any unsightly weeds. In the bright clarity of August, she saw that his grave was completely surrounded by brilliant yellow sunflowers. For a second Angie thought about chopping them down, but in their slow turning to face the sun, she saw something holy. In each large, round flower, she saw the destruction and rebirth of her Indian race. In each yellow orb she saw the love of the Great Spirit. In each sunflower, she saw the smiling face of Sherman.

Bobo Murders Mickey Mouse

The day was cold for late August. The two tribal members named Bobo and Paulie shivered as they hunkered into the battered pickup truck. They drove around in circles in Pine Ridge Village trying to decide where they could get some hot coffee to warm their bones. Bobo Robidoux and Paulie Roan Horse were business associates and first cousins. Mostly they were trappers, which meant that they sold hides and spotlighted deer. Sometimes when game was sparse, they drove their old truck along the roads collecting beer cans to sell as scrap aluminum.

"Well, what about Big Bat's Conoco?" Bobo asked Paulie. Bobo was dark, had a crew cut and weighed three hundred pounds. Paulie was light-skinned and wore braids.

"I got zee, flat-ass broke," said Paulie. "And besides, I don't like the coff they make in there. It's too weak. I gotta have cowboy coff."

"Weak or not, I ain't too cashy either," Bobo said.

"Well, caffeine ain't good for us noways," Paulie said. "It raises blood pressure and stuff, makes you nervous in the service."

Then, as if on cue, terror struck and elevated their blood pressures. A tribal police unit with sirens flashing and lights strobing skidded to a halt next to the pickup. The two men watched as a burly, surly Indian cop squeezed out from behind the steering wheel. It was Captain Wilmer Ten Dogs. He was tall, six-six, and weighed in at nearly three hundred fifty pounds. He adjusted the holster on his .357 Magnum as he slowly waddled toward the truck.

Bobo was relieved. Ten Dogs was one of the few guys on the reservation he could stand next to and feel skinny. As Bobo rolled down the window to talk to the cop, he caught a glimpse of Paulie out of the corner of his eye. Paulie looked like the canary who just swallowed the cat. *Something's wrong,* Bobo thought.

"*Hau,* how's it going, Officer Dogs?" Bobo greeted the cop. Captain Ten Dogs stood erect and sneered at Bobo but said nothing. Bobo stared back but could only see his own face in the mirrored glasses the cop wore. Then the tribal cop lashed his fist through the open window and popped Bobo on the shoulder. With an evil laugh, Ten Dogs took off his sunglasses and stared directly into Bobo's shivering eyeballs.

"So tell me, how much is mice hides going for these days? And can you tell me the price of eggs?" the cop snickered. Bobo glared at Paulie. Paulie had his head hung low.

"You're a butthead, Paulie."

"I ain't done nothing, Bo."

"You betrayed me, Paulie," Bobo said in a low, angry voice. "I didn't think you would, but you really are the King of the Blabbermouths."

"Man, when those White tourists come on the Rez looking for a hunting safari, I'm gonna point them your way," Ten

Dogs said and roared. "Bobo Robidoux, the great White hunter."

Bobo snapped his eyes away from the cop, rolled up the window, put the truck in gear, and peeled out. As he drove by the dilapidated Sioux Nation Shopping Center, he stopped the truck.

"See those *tahansis* shooting the bull over there?" he asked Paulie, pointing to a motley crew of loiterers. "Here's where your ass gets out. You might as well join the rest of the reservation gossipers."

"Those are just winos over there. Why should I go hang out with them?" Paulie asked.

"Ain't that Mariana Two Knives sitting there? Geez, man, go check it out. Maybe she'll give you some. I heard she puts out for cash."

"I don't wanna hang out with stinky winos, I'm telling you," Paulie whined and stared down at his scruffy cowboy boots.

"Yeah, you do. You got about as much honor as them," Bobo said with a snarl. "See you."

"I'm sorry," Paulie said.

"Get your sorry ass outta my truck," Bobo said and spit out the window. "Take a hike. I ain't got no use for tattletales."

Paulie got out of the truck with a hangdog, truly dejected look on his mug. He wondered how he could have stooped so low as to betray his best friend. Sure, he had gotten a little tilted in the Long Branch Bar in Heinzville the week before, and Ten Dogs the cop *had* been in there. But had he actually told him the story? He couldn't remember if he had or not. But he clearly recalled the day of terror that had prompted the cop to ask Bobo about the mice and eggs.

They had been out hunting that day and checking the traps they'd put out several days before. They were on tribal land and doing the same routines as their ancestors had done for centuries. They were putting bacon on the table.

It had been a rough morning already. They had shot a gaunt coyote that looked like it had a bad case of mange. Its pelt would be worth next to nothing from the fur trader who visited the Rez every two weeks during the winter. And to add insult to injury, after they had thrown the carcass into the bed of the truck, it had miraculously come back to life. Some of these damn coyotes on the Rez had more lives than a cat.

Bobo was driving, as usual, and for some unknown reason Paulie turned his head around to look out the back window. When Paulie peered through the glass, he found he was face to face with a slobbering, grinning coyote. Not knowing what else to do, Paulie panicked and screamed. Bobo was so startled that he followed suit and screamed too, but not before he levitated from the seat and boinged his head a good one on the truck's ceiling. What's worse was he soiled his shorts— Paulie's screaming had startled him that badly.

"Screw a gnu!" Bobo screeched and hit the brakes, making the truck skid to a halt off the road and halfway into a stand of wild cherry. "What the holy hell is going on, Paulie? You made me pass liquid gas."

"The coyote's alive," Paulie stammered. Bobo gave him the evil eye and got out of the truck to look. By the time he reached the back of the vehicle, the coyote had hightailed it out of there.

"There he is," yelled Paulie, pointing at the distant creature bounding over a faraway hill. "That's one motivatin' critter."

Bobo was still thinking of the goofy look of terror on Paulie's face as they approached a stand of cottonwoods in the Medicine Root District of the Rez, where their small line of traps had been set. He was not so amused that Paulie's scream had brought forth a scream from him too. Sometimes Paulie made him feel like they were a redskin version of Abbott and Costello.

As they approached the first of their boxlike traps, they heard a noise but could see nothing since the trap had been carefully hidden beneath the boughs of a low-riding pine tree.

"Something's in there," Paulie whispered. "And you stink."

"Tell me something I don't know," Bobo said with clenched teeth. "Go check it out, Paulie."

"No, you check it out," Paulie murmured, still thinking of the Houdini coyote that had just escaped.

"Chicken," Bobo said scornfully.

"Better chicken than have to change my shorts like you," Paulie said and instantly regretted his words. Bobo's eyes shot flames of anger.

"Here's the easy way to do it," Bobo said and pointed his twelve-gauge Remington at the clump of pine. He fired two rounds point-blank at the exact place where the trap stood. Pine needles, wire mesh, and other debris flew in all directions. The two Indian trappers slowly crept toward their trap. They both squinted and peered inside.

"Oh, my God," yelled Paulie. "It's a . . . it's a damn mouse!"

"A mouse . . . mouse?" Bobo echoed and grimaced as he surveyed his mangled trap. "Mouse?" he asked again, not quite believing the dance of the word upon his tongue.

"M-I-C-K-E-Y-M-O-U-S-E," Paulie sang the Mouseketeers' song. "Should we have him stuffed and mounted?" he tittered, teasing Bobo as they walked to their next trap, a quarter of a mile from there. "There ain't much left of him, though," Paulie roared. "You killed Mickey friggin' Mouse!" Bobo did not answer his friend. It was turning into a bad day.

They approached their second trap. In this one they had used a live chicken as bait for anything that might be hungry, be it coyote, badger, fox, or whatever. The chicken was plump and finger-licking good, a hen whose egg-laying powers had been lost somewhere in the ozone.

"Watch out for mice," Paulie laughed as Bobo walked angrily up to the trap. Bobo cursed and kicked at the ground. The chicken was still inside, alive as they were.

"Hey, look at that," Paulie yelled and danced around the cage. "It laid an egg. It laid an egg. The son of a bitch done give us an egg."

Bobo reached in and retrieved the egg and then hoisted the cage-trap containing the chicken into the back of the pickup. Paulie was still snickering to himself. Bobo shook his head and walked up to Paulie. Without a word, he took the egg and smashed it on top of Paulie's head. Then they got into the truck and drove back to Pine Ridge Village without another word.

Bobo dropped Paulie off at his house. "You tell anybody about today, Paulie, and you're going to be King of the Blabbermouths," Bobo told him. "I don't want this getting out on the Moccasin Telegraph."

"Well, I sure don't want to be King of the Blabbermouths," Paulie said. "But still, you had no reason to crack my head with a egg."

"I was just trying to add some protein to your tiny brain," Bobo said and laughed for the first time that day. "See you, *kola*."

Paulie shook his head and went in his house. He took a hot shower and washed the egg out of his hair. Then he debated who would be the first person he would tell about how Bobo shot the mouse. And how Bobo had pooped in his pants.

The Night Beans
Talked to Old Bear

It had been a long, hard day for Old Bear. Not a single thing had gone right at his new job, and all day long he'd suffered because a filling had fallen out of one of his front teeth. A throbbing hole the size of the Grand Canyon made for a miserable day. He'd eaten nothing but aspirin and coffee for the entire work shift, and then he went home to his cave and directly to bed without supper.

He fell asleep immediately, but then was awakened around midnight when his hellacious toothache got lonesome. He took more aspirin and even placed a chunk of one directly inside the cavity, knowing that you're not supposed to do that. Then he flopped back to bed and waited for the pain to subside.

When it did, he still couldn't sleep. He was ravenously hungry. Visions of food danced in his head and made him drool. He pictured juicy venison steaks, banana creme pies, pepperoni pizza, fry-bread tacos, and even the noodle casserole he had once made for Coyote.

Determined not to do anything that might aggravate his tooth, Old Bear thrashed atop his bed and tried to quit thinking of food. When he was younger, any insomnia he had was quickly quelled with sweet thoughts of women. And more often than not, there was a cuddly female bear in bed next to him. Now that he was far past his prime and not all that interested in females, all he could think of was food when he wanted a distraction. Deliriously hungry, he now went so far as to visualize the strange types of food he had seen his friends eat over the years.

Once, in the '60s, he had gone through a period when he'd grown his hair long and taken to wearing sandals. He moved from the High Plains to San Francisco, where he lived with an Arapaho woman who worked as a stripper in North Beach. Her name was Lavina, and Lavina's high point in dining was to go down to a nearby fish and chips place, buy a large order, take them home, and drown them with Miracle Whip before devouring them. Old Bear didn't stay with her for very long.

Many of his friends had peculiar culinary habits. The oddest of his pals was Raven. Old Bear and Raven had batched together during the messy period after Old Bear's first divorce. It was a time of serious drinking and skirt chasing, a time long before Raven developed his taste for haute cuisine and abusing women.

For breakfast, Raven would very often take a slice of white bread, butter it, then peck out a hole in the center. He would fry it in a skillet and just when it started to brown, he would drop an egg into the hole he'd created. When this concoction was done, he would cover the entire mess with strawberry jam and eat it. The recollection of this culinary delight always sent Old Bear's stomach into spasms of anarchy and revulsion. Bears have a nasty sweet tooth.

Raven was also the first one to show him the peculiar joys of *menudo*. *Menudo*, that spicy tripe soup that Chicanos and some Indians were so fond of, was a far cry from *taniga*, the traditional tripe soup of the Sioux that Old Bear was quite familiar with. Old Bear eventually did develop a taste for *menudo* and found it was most excellent for hangovers. While he wasn't exactly big on eating the innards of mammals, *menudo* became one of his all-time favorites.

Tripe soup was one of the few internal-organ dishes he would eat. He could still remember his own grandfather Great Bear frying up a skillet of cow brains for breakfast. The very memory made Old Bear retch. He never liked tongue, heart, brains, although he would eat liver and onions and sometimes would treat himself to liverwurst lunch meat. He sure as hell had never eaten "mountain oysters" and never would. The very thought of them made him cross his legs and wince.

Old Bear stretched on his bed and scratched his own oysters, and at that moment he noticed that his tooth pain had miraculously vanished. He rolled over and allowed his brain to continue bombarding his stomach with visions of food. He never was big on ketchup, but now even the thought of just plain ketchup made his mouth water. His first wife, a bear woman, used to drench everything she ate in ketchup. From baked potatoes to bacon, from tuna fish sandwiches to toast in the morning, she ate everything swimming in ketchup. Her name was Mountain Bear Woman and she hailed from the hills near Lame Deer, Montana.

Mountain Bear Woman ate ketchup on Spam and ketchup on spaghetti. Bear only rarely used ketchup, sometimes a little on a burger or a dab on his French fries, but his first wife was a ketchup freak. Mountain Bear Woman even ate plain ketchup sandwiches. Old Bear was sure that her peculiar diet played a part in his decision to divorce her. Plus she was screwing around with a White cowboy.

And so, into the night, he lay spasming on the bed dreaming of food. He had come from a very poor family of ten cubs, but there were still some foods he would not eat as an adult. He hated the concoction of macaroni, hamburger, and tomato sauce that the humans called "American chop suey." He would no longer eat peas from a can. Or creamed corn. He would not eat Spam or processed American cheese. Spam and cheese sandwiches had been a family staple when he was growing up.

Nevertheless, his own mother always made her own bread, and he remembered how in grade school he would trade sandwiches with his buddies so he could have some of that wondrous "Wonder Bread." Now he salivated copiously at the mere thought of his mother's bread. He pictured the steaming loaves, fresh from the oven, with hand-churned butter drizzled over the top of them. The yeasty memory made rivulets of drool dribble down his chin. Sometimes the good old days really were the good old days.

"Ah, Mom, you made good bread," he said in semi-prayer. His mother had gone to the spirit world many years before.

His family had had a cow named Bossie when he was growing up. He used to have to milk her morning and night, and thus to this day he had always preferred the milk that came in cartons. The milk taken directly from the cow tasted too wild and reminded him of the liberties he had taken with Bossie one warm summer night when his raging groin grew hungry. And he loved homemade butter. He would take Bossie's cream, put it in a jar, and shake it until it turned to butter. Then he would take the congealed cream and press it through a cheesecloth. Her butter was most excellent.

Bear dreamed on about food, sweet, delicious food. Food thoughts were running rampant through his soul. He still had a fondness for fry bread, but he liked it cooked in a skillet rather than deep-fried. One of his nieces had a constant craving for peanut butter and banana sandwiches, which he thought a little weird, but he recalled chunky peanut butter and maple syrup sandwiches. And when things were lean during his childhood, his mother would make sandwiches out of lard sprinkled with sugar.

He pictured his mother's stew. The family seemed to live on stew, and he always figured a bear could live on a good beef stew and little else. When he was a teenager, he would butter two slices of bread and put cold stew leftovers between them—a stew sandwich. He even took stew sandwiches to school.

"You ain't lived until you've eaten a cold stew sandwich," he told Raven one night when they were in a cowboy bar, drunk, womanless, and starving for any hint of something feminine.

"Give me corn chowder any day," Raven said.

"Forget that. Cold stew sandwiches rule."

"You mammals got your head up your—"

"No, man, I'm telling you. There's nothing in the world that can compare to a cold stew sandwich on a hot summer day."

"Bear breath, you're dead wrong," Raven had informed him. "You ain't had nothing till you try a potato chip and pickle sandwich or, better yet, strawberry jam and mayonnaise on wheat toast."

"Hmmm," Old Bear said and ordered them more beers.

Old Bear could relate to the jam and mayo sandwich. One of his supreme favorites was leftover turkey made into sandwiches with mayonnaise and cranberry sauce—the jellied kind, not the stuff with real live cranberries dancing around in it. It was the thought of this particular sandwich that made Thanksgiving a pleasant memory. And mincemeat pie—oh, sexually sweet mincemeat pie!

And so, as he tossed and turned in his dream palace of food, it was inevitable that his mind would dredge up the highest form of food known to bears and mankind—beans!

Old Bear loved beans in any form. He drooled over ham hocks and lima beans, butter beans and sausage, canned pork and beans, chili beans, refried beans, Cajun red beans and rice, and just plain kidney beans spiced up with bacon and onion. He was mad about any form of the "musical fruit," from bean sandwiches to bean soup, from barbecued beans to three-bean salad. He was a freak for nachos slathered with bean dip. He was mad for navy bean soup.

In fact, he thought that if the United States government would forget nuclear reactors or Iranian oil for a while and concentrate on harnessing the power of the bean, then Mother Earth might just be around a little longer—not that he was an environmentalist or anything.

And why couldn't the pencil pushers at the Pentagon devise a machine gun that fired cooked beans? Or a bazooka that launched bean burritos? Maybe, Old Bear thought, in that way the cruel stupidity that mankind was so fond of, that Godless tragedy they called war, would never amount to much more than a hill of beans.

And so Old Bear's mind continued to rage on at the same time his stomach growled and whined. In the middle of the night, because of a toothache, he began thinking of food and made a thought bridge from beans to nuclear energy. And was he ever hungry! He was truly starving to death on his bed. He dreamed of being buried alive in a steaming mountain of pinto beans and buttered bread.

At two-thirty in the morning, somewhere in that nebulous region between sleep and waking, Old Bear began to hear strange voices coming from his refrigerator. He knew who was speaking to him. It was a pot of leftover kidney beans chattering in the chilly depths of the fridge.

"Come and get us," they said.

Old Bear sat up in bed and lit a cigarette and smiled.

"Come and get us," the pot of beans repeated.

"Okay, damn it, you asked for it," he said and stood up.

Old Bear got dressed and attacked the pot of beans. He was hungry, ever so hungry, and his badass toothache was long gone. *It's wonderful,* he thought, *to live alone and to be kind and caring to yourself.* And he sat at his kitchen table and ate and ate and stared out the window at the twinkling stars. They were as numerous as the beans in the pot he held. The recently deceased beans in his stomach were just beginning to release their souls. Old Bear became Heaven. Old Bear became God. Old Bear became the nacreous gas of space before the Big Bang.

Auntie Angie's
Cheyenne Affair

Three years since I seen that girl Mariana and I guess it's high time to find her. Timmy John Pretty Bull, he say he seen her up in Montana, in the city of Billings and I say what's she doing up there and he say, well, you know, drinking and stuff. So when I find out he's headed for Crow Fair to fancy dance, I ask him to drive me and I'll catch a bus into Billings. I guess it's high time to find that girl, I tell him.

"I doubt she's gonna want to come home," he say.

"Why you say that?" I ask him.

"Well," he say, "if she wanted to be down here in South Dakota, then she wouldn't be up there."

"Hummppphhh," I say. Sometimes talking to that boy is like talking to a television set. The set it don't hear you and it say things that don't make much sense. And some of those programs laugh to themselves over something not funny. That's how that boy is. Sometimes he just let out a high giggle for no reason.

"Well, it's up to you," he say and shake his head and let out a young pony whinny-giggle.

Well, I tell him, yes, it *sure* is up to me and he say okay and we go. It's warm, too warm out, and there's a lot of dead skunks on the road when we leave the Rez, go to Rapid City, and then north on Interstate 90 into Wyoming and towards Montana. A good thing his car radio work, but that boy only play what you call rap and it don't make no sense to me.

Seven hours later, Timmy John drive me from Crow Agency to Hardin for me to catch the bus. Last time I was up here many years ago, them Crow Indians stacked like cordwood outside the bars. And here they are again. A shame to be seen that way and only a few miles from Big Horn Battlefield and all them tourists looking for a whiff of something noble Indian. Well, that's what they get for siding with the *wasicu* against us Sioux and Cheyenne. Damn them anyways.

And damn that Mariana for running away, I'm thinking when I see all those drunk Crows. Oh, it's sad to be an old woman. Sad to be sixty-three, but I ain't dead yet, so it's even sadder to be looking for my niece Mariana. Thank God I got my AA to keep me sane. And I got one of their books with me in case I feel weak and need some good words.

She's just a kid, sure, almost twenty even if she already had two babies she adopted out besides Sherman who died. And here Timmy John said he seen her all drunked up in the bars in downtown Billings. Said that's where to look. And that she looked pretty rough and all like some kinda tramp. I didn't like him saying *that,* but at least he's a honest boy even though he does drink. Well, he don't drink no more than anybody else. These kids these days. They make ancestor spirits cry.

And so I ride the bus to Billings. There's some Indians, maybe Cheyennes, on the bus, but I don't look at them. I got things on my mind. This ain't no joyride and I ain't on vacation. When the bus pull into the station, it is starting getting dark and all the lights of the city is coming on. The streets full of traffic from all the people going home from work, whatever kind of work they all do downtown Billings. It sure is a big city and it don't look too friendly.

So I tie my old blue scarf on my head, get out with my shoulder bag and purse, and go looking for Mariana, damn her drunk hide. Timmy John he say all them bars downtown is all close together and not too far from the bus station and that's where to look if he was me. And here by the time I make it to the first bar, it is now pitch-black out and this bar only has a small blinking Budweiser sign on it, no name far as I can see. There is a young Indian boy standing in front of the door, blocking it.

"Nephew," I say, "is this where all the Skins hang out?"

"I ain't your nephew, old lady," he say real rude to me. Well, what a little bitch *he* is. And dressed in a leather vest and tight Levi's, and wearing dark glasses at night. His black hair is short and all greased back.

"What tribe are you?" I ask him and wonder if his whole damn tribe be as rude as him.

"Tribe? Whaddya mean tribe? I ain't no damn *Indio*. I'm a Chicano, Mama. From Denver."

Well, I almost want to slap him and ask don't Chicanos teach their children to respect elders, but I don't. He really make me mad. And don't he know that Mexicans are Indians too. Where does he think his brown skin come from? Eating too many bean burritos? Oh, this boy he make me mad, but I just ask him if there is many Indians inside the bar. If there is any young Indian girls.

"Oh, so that's what you're looking for," he say and chuckle and then raise his eyes to the sky. He don't know it, but he is sure close to getting his Taco lips slapped good.

"Well, yes I am," I say. "One about twenty, good-looking. Long black hair down to her waist."

"Damn," he say. "You lezzies got an appetite even when you're elderly," and laughs and stands aside from the door. I don't know what he mean, but I walk in and am I surprised. There's guys dancing with guys. And here they are kissing each other too. Most are dressed in leather. This is a *winkte* bar. It's like I opened a trapdoor to hell. I can't believe it. They can't believe me either. They all stare at me like I'm the one just came in from outer space and not them.

"Is there something you need?" a big muscleman with tattoos all over his arms ask me. Well, there is lots of things I need, but I don't have time to give him my list. He's wearing rhinestone earrings and cowboy chaps of black leather. I can't take my eyes off them chaps and earrings. Geez, what is wrong with these people anyways.

"Well, I'm looking for my niece, name Mariana Two Knives," I say and try to keep from giggling at his chaps. I want to ask him if he going to a rodeo later tonight, but I bite my lips. No sense in being rude like them.

"Two Knives? Try the next bar up the block. That's where all the war whoops congregate for prayer services," he says.

"War whoops?" I ask. *War whoops?*

"Yeah, you know, those of the Native American Indian persuasion. War whoops—like you."

"Thanks, Tattoo," I say to this jackass and turn and leave the *winkte* bar not a minute too soon. "I hope you don't get bucked off easy tonight," I say and wink but he just give me a blank stare like my putdown ain't even stuck to him. As I'm heading out the door, two boys on the dance floor are starting to fight, screaming like women and trying to scratch each other's eyes out. Now I seen it all, I think. Now I seen it all . . .

But I sure ain't. Walking to the next bar, I see a street full of prostitutes. Shaking their rear ends, waving at traffic and such. I know what they are and they're Indian too. I start to walk up to one to ask about Mariana, but when I do, this

young girl I approach glance quick at me then turn her eyes.
I can tell she is shamed.

"Excuse me," I say.

"I'm too busy," she say, chewing gum not even looking at
me when she talks. She is close to Mariana's age.

"I'm looking for someone," I say and just then she snap her
eyes and walk away before I can even finish what I'm saying.
What is the matter with these kids these days? Damn, if she
so shamed out about what she is doing then she shouldn't be
doing it.

"I'm gonna tell your family," I say at her rapidly moving
backside even though I don't know her family. "I know your
mother and father," I lie. When I say that, she start to run. I
don't know. Maybe I'm being too mean to the poor child. She
look like a Cheyenne girl. Probably from Lame Deer. I keep
going towards the other bar when a man's voice come out of
the darkness.

"Who you looking for, Grandmother?"

"Huh," I say and turn around. "Grandmother?" I say when
I see the man is close to my age. "Grandmother?"

"Who are you looking for?" the man say again. I squint my
eyes and see he's a middle-aged Indian man with short hair
and bad, bad complexion. He is wearing a green suit coat, a
clean white shirt, and baggy Levi's. His pimply face got a straw
Stetson squatting on top of it.

"My niece Mariana Two Knives," I say. "Who are you
anyways?"

"Richard Tall Elk," he tell me. "Cheyenne."

Well, at least I'm a little relieved he ain't no Crow Indian. I
tell him my name and tell him where I'm from. He tell me
he's been to Pine Ridge, he might know my relatives, and
then ask me if I can buy him a drink.

"Sure could use one, if you don't mind," he say.

"Well, I do mind because I'm in AA," I tell him. "But if you help me look for my niece, I'll give you two dollars."

"Yeah, sure I'll help you," he say. "Best place to look is right up this street here. Come on. I'll take you in and introduce you around. Lots of wild Indians in there."

"Well, I didn't come up here just to gander at drunk Indians and I don't like the idea of going into these bars. I'm still recovering," I tell him just so he know I ain't some tramp or something.

"You want to preach me that AA stuff or you want to find your niece?" he ask and keep walking. I follow. He don't seem dangerous or sneaky like some drunks.

"Never heard of her," a strange, fat, bald Indian gent in the bar where we first go tell us. Well, nothing to do but go down the row of barstools and ask until someone say something I want to hear. And halfway down, I hear something I have come to hear.

"Yeah, I know Mariana," a young girl about twenty or so say when I ask her. She is dressed good, wears glasses, and I wonder how come she is in this stinky saloon.

"Mariana went back to Rapid City just yesterday," she say.
"You her friend?" I ask.

"Not really," she say. "We just covered some of the same territory. Drank together and stuff. I know her pretty good."

Territory, I think and then I wonder if Mariana been out on the street selling her fanny like these other Indian girls. I hope not. I say a silent prayer and give this Tall Elk guy the two dollars like I promised. One thing, I am not an Indian giver. Thanks, he tell me and he scoot out the door fast as can be, the poor thirsty thing.

"See you," I say, then I leave too, walking the direction back to the bus station.

On the way there, not one minute after I leave that bar, is this same Cheyenne guy and two young Blacks, *hasapas,* is talking to him. Both them wearing them silly, baggy-bloomer shorts. I am walking towards them and soon I can hear the Indian guy say that he don't got no money and to leave him alone. And here one of the black guys, maybe seventeen years old, he shove this Richard Tall Elk down to the ground real hard.

"Hey," I yell. "Leave that man alone." Both of them are trying to go through his pockets while he is on the sidewalk. In the darkness, they look like black wolves ripping chunks of flesh off some poor deer or something. It is scaring me. "Help," I yell and look around but nobody is there to help. And one of the blacks he leap up and run towards me.

Next thing I know he is trying to punch me with one hand while his other is trying to steal my purse. I am kicking and yelling and trying to hit him back with my free hand. Some of the things I am saying are bad, bad cusswords, but even those don't stop him. It become clear to me that I am dealing with the devil, even if his skin is black.

For a second his hand release my purse and I am swinging it to his cruel head. It smacks solid, *clunk*. His eyes go blank, so I do it again and again. *Clunk, clunk,* and then *crack*. His nose gushing blood and I don't feel no pity for him. Then his Black buddy is helping him escape down some alleyway. And nobody left on the Billings street but me and the Cheyenne man. His nose is bleeding too and he stand up shaking from fear. He is crying and so I start too.

"They got my two dollars," he say.

"That ain't nothing," I tell him. "At least we're alive. They coulda cut our throats. What's the matter with them anyways. Lord, don't they have no respect for old people?"

"Naw," he say. "They don't respect nothing, even themselves. There didn't use to be none of them around here. Now these past couple years a whole bunch of coloreds move up from Denver, L.A., whatever. This place is dangerous now at night. They don't care. And it ain't only Blacks. It's the Mexicans, the Indians, the Whites too. They'll kill you and take your money, these young ones. This the third time this year I got rolled by young boys. And not only that, they sell dope to the Indians, like Indians ain't got enough trouble handling just booze."

"Damn them anyways," I say. "What's the matter with those Blacks? No wonder those cops beat up that Rodney King."

"Honest, it ain't only the Black ones," he say. "Some of these Indians and Mexicans just as bad, if not worse," he say and take my hand. "You talk to any Indian in Billings. Damn hard to live on skid row anymore."

"Why you doing that?" I ask and nod with my lips toward his big hand holding mine.

"You saved my life," he say and then he give me a big hug. We is still both shaking, but then his hug start to feel good. And I am so glad I got an Indian man to hold me in this cement jungle.

"They took your money," I say.

"Yeah," he say and shrug his shoulders.

"Come on," I say. "I'm gonna buy you a drink or two. You look like you need it after what you just been through. Now don't expect me to drink with you. I'll just sit next to you and read my AA book."

He look at me and smile and say, "Then I guess you don't got nothing against us Cheyenne?"

"Why should I?" I say. "You *Sihiyelas* were with us at Little Big Horn weren't you? You held our horses didn't you?"

"Billings ain't the Little Big Horn," he say and laugh. Then he tell me I am a nice woman and my face blush a little. I tell him come on, I ain't got all night to sit with him. I gotta be back at the bus station before midnight.

"I'll buy you three drinks," I say. "Me, I'm just gonna drink a Coke and read my book. Come on, let's go."

"Fine," he say.

"That's what I thought," I say. Even if he is a wino, he smell clean and soapy like he just took a bath. We is walking back up to the Indian bar and I look at him good when we come under a lamp. He is like me. When he was young, I bet he was one good-looking war whoop. And I feel young, younger than I felt in years. And more than that, I'm starting to get that old, real warm feeling, if you know what I mean.

Abducted by Aliens
Inside Her Brain

Rapid City, South Dakota. A week before Christmas. Bitter, bleak, freezing, the white-trash citizenry hauled inside by the bitter cold. Late in the afternoon, Mariana watched the fat snowflakes slowly drift through the gray sky. Inside the downtown bus depot, poor people and students were scurrying to make connections home. Mariana was not homeward bound at all, but was only warming up, her feet swollen spongy and painful from bum-hiking the icy streets.

She had a shimmering hangover and her clothes smelled funky with grease, booze, and puke. Her eyes were red and the people in the bus station avoided making eye contact with her. When she lifted a half-smoked cigarette from a sand-filled ashtray and lit it, she was relieved that it didn't taste halfway bad. Even if it had tasted bad, she would have smoked it anyways. She had almost reached the bottom in her delirious descent into self-destruction. The blissful sewers of hell or some alien dimension beckoned. Sometimes, she told herself, she felt as if she had been cursed by being born an Indian.

Mariana was thinking about Charlie Boy Red Blanket and how she was glad she had left him. He beat her too much. He'd even hit her for calling him "Charlie Boy," although that was what all his friends and family called him. He demanded that he be addressed as "Charles," especially when he was drunk. And he was drunk all the time and bitter, crazy-mean during their last days together. His brain was poached in fire water.

"Only my buds call me Charlie Boy," he had shouted and then slapped her on three separate occasions.

And yet almost every time he got drunk, he would sit for hours and call her "Mariana banana, Mariana banana." Drunker yet, he would mumble, "Mariana ramma lamma ding-dong." If she gave the slightest hint of being offended, he would smack her. Mariana had come to view men as one of the great evils of the world—men, snakes, and breast cancer.

"I thought you loved me," Mariana would cry when he abused her. "I thought you loved me. This ain't love."

On one of his drunken binges, Charlie Boy had his friends shave his head like Charles Barkley and he'd kept it shaved for that whole year. He dressed in baggy clothes like an urban Black gangster and that puzzled Mariana, but she was too scared of him to ever ask him about his taste in clothes or culture. Even when he walked around with his cap turned backwards, she said nothing. Charlie Boy was tall, dark, extremely muscular and had scary eyes. She didn't dare cross him. You can never tell what a liquor-addicted fullblood man might do next, Mariana had told her Indian girlfriends.

"You got that right," every one of them had said at one time or another. "Don't *even* have to be a fullblood to be crazy," they added.

That last month with him, Mariana completely lost track of the beatings. They came often and were severe. A distant corner of her consciousness whispered that it was only a matter of time before he did the job right and killed her.

He came home drunk from an indoor rodeo at the Rapid City Civic Center one afternoon and screamed at her to "kill them black ants any time you see 'em." Mariana thought that was a goofy thing to say. She figured she was expected to laugh so she giggled. Charlie Boy backhanded her and then kicked her in the shin with his stinky Air Jordans. She was still writhing on the floor when he staggered out the door.

"What'd I do?" she whimpered long after he was gone. "Dear God damn it all, what the hell did I do?"

The next morning he stumbled in and asked her to cook him some fried eggs and potatoes. He was contrite and hungover and he apologized. He had a black eye and his shirt was torn. "Them black ants ain't ants," he explained. "They're carpenter ants and they're eating the fuckin' foundation of this house. Don't you know nothing?"

Mariana was unsure whether to shake her head yes or no, so she simply nodded and began to cook his breakfast, afraid of saying anything lest they be the wrong words. She wondered why he cared about the house. It was a dump anyway. It wasn't even theirs, and Hank Goldberg the landlord never fixed anything that needed fixing. Goldberg, the grossly fat, blackhead-nosed landlord, had said she could do him some favors the next time she was late with the rent. She knew better than to tell Charlie Boy about *that.* No sense in getting beat up because of a horny landlord.

"Friggin' termites *and* ants can eat your foundation and stuff," Charlie Boy said, burped, and then went into the living room and passed out on the couch. Mariana spent the entire day cleaning house and watching out for termites or ants. She never saw a single one.

That afternoon, he awoke and asked for an early dinner. They ate sloppy joes and fried potatoes and then sat together watching television for an hour. Then he got dressed and left the house without saying where he was going. Late that night Charlie Boy returned lopsided, with his cruel eyes halfway rolled back in his head.

He came home like a devil in the middle of a tremendous thunderstorm. Lightning lashed out across the Great Plains trying to electrocute the Dakotas. The storm had knocked out the electricity, and Charlie Boy had fallen in the darkness of the front yard and lost his glasses. He banged on the door and made Mariana join him on her hands and knees on the wet, unmowed grass helping him search for his glasses.

"Find the damn things before lightning zaps us," he yelled.

"I wish it would," she mumbled as low as she could.

"Keep lookin', bitch."

Mariana would never forget that night as long as she lived. The torrential rains had brought hundreds upon hundreds of foot-long nightcrawlers to the surface and her knees were soon covered with mashed worm flesh. She prayed for the lightning to strike them both dead. She gagged at the thought of those thrashing, slimy worms dying under her brown flesh, but she never complained. Wormy knees were better than Charlie Boy's fists. Almost anything was better than getting beat up.

"I don't find them damn glasses then I'm really gonna be pissed," Charlie Boy had shouted at her.

"I'm looking," she said in a voice that was barely more than a whisper. "I'm looking."

"You damn well better be looking," he said. "I don't find them I'm gonna knock the piss outta you."

Mariana had nodded and scooted quickly over the grass, smashing scores of worms before she located what they were searching for. She handed the glasses to Charlie Boy and he walked inside without even acknowledging her.

"Thanks for nothing," she had mumbled when she was sure he was out of hearing range. Then she too went inside and made plans to leave him. It was either that or kill him and that drunken shit-shorts wasn't worth going to jail for. Two weeks later, she packed two plastic shopping bags and left him in the middle of the night without a good-bye.

For a few days she stayed with her old boyfriend Verdell Ten Bears until his AWOL woman came home. Nine days after she moved out, she got the news that Charlie Boy had gotten his skull bashed by an aluminum baseball bat wielded by an unknown assailant outside an Indian bar. He was permanently paralyzed, but Mariana had no intention of ever visiting him at Sioux San Hospital. Mariana suspected Verdell Ten Bears had done her that favor.

Late in the afternoon, when the crowd of travelers thinned and only a few derelicts and students remained in the bus station, Mariana got up and checked the coin cups on a row of pay phones and found nothing. She shrugged, coughed and hocked a loogie onto the green terrazzo floor and walked to the ladies' room. It reeked of Lysol and urine.

In front of a sparkling-clean mirror, she surveyed the ravages the passage of time had left on her young face. It had been five years since Sherman had died and four years since she'd had her tubes tied at the PHS hospital. She was now twenty-one and could drink legally, although she had done so anyway since she was thirteen. She needed a drink badly. She was beginning to hurt from the unpleasant creature of sobriety that was slowly quickening inside her body.

Mariana crawled under the doorway of a pay toilet and took off her jeans and removed her panties. She put her jeans back on and walked out the door, putting a small wad of toilet paper in the latch so it wouldn't close and she could get back in. She filled a sink with hot soapy water and washed out her underwear. Mariana held the panties under a hot-air hand dryer until they were no longer damp. Then she wet a red bandanna and went back into the stall to take a sponge bath.

She took a brush from her purse and pulled out the snarls in her short black hair. She even found an old tube of cherry lip balm and applied it to her cracked lips, although her aim was off and her mouth looked lopsided. Mariana Two Knives put on the black leather jacket a biker she'd slept with gave her and wiped some dried crud off the sleeves. She took a deep breath and walked back to the lobby and sat back down on a bench.

She rubbed her face and felt a pimple near her nose. She squeezed it between two fingers until it popped. She ground the white pulp until it disappeared and then walked up to an old man who looked like the last cowboy on earth.

The last cowboy seemed vaguely familiar, but then all *wasicus* looked the same to her. He looked exactly like Ross Perot's twin, and he was doing a crossword puzzle in a small booklet. Mariana interrupted his attempt at literacy and bummed a cigarette. The old wrangler had a *pachuco* tattoo on the webbing between his thumb and forefinger. Mariana had one there too, although hers was homemade with a pocketknife and ballpoint pen. She had done it during her first jail time for public drunkenness.

The last cowboy said he lived in Rapid City and was headed up to Deadwood to do some gambling in the dorky casinos there. His bus wasn't due to leave for another hour and he offered to buy Mariana a drink or two. She thanked him and declined and went back to her own bench. Sometimes life struck her so strangely that she was convinced that she'd been abducted and made crazy by space aliens. Aliens might even be living in her own brain. She looked down at her own *pachuco* tattoo. The cross with three sun rays above it gave her a slight twinge of hope.

Something in the blood of her people worshiped the sun. It was something that the modern age could not destroy. The Lakota were children of *Wi*, the sun. A ray of sunshine illuminated the bus depot. The winter sun had broken through clouds and she knew this was a sign. Mariana knew then that she had to go down to the detox center and turn herself in for the cure one more time. It was always hard but she would do it. She had to. She stared at the last cowboy across the way and focused her eyes on the tattoo on his weathered white hand. The spoked rays above the cross pulled her to her feet and she walked over to him.

"Can I bum another cigarette?" she asked.

"You're too young to smoke," he teased.

"No, I'm legal. Let me have one more smoke, please? I'm having a damn nicotine fit like you wouldn't believe."

"Sure, sure you can have one more," he said and reached into his coat pocket and pulled out a pack of Marlboros. Strapped to the pack of cigarettes with a green rubber band was a wad of twenty-dollar bills. A thick wad. A wad thicker than Mariana had ever seen outside of television or in the possession of a crack dealer.

"You still offering to buy me that drink?" Mariana asked. Her mouth actually began to water from the mere sight of the cowboy's money.

"Listen, sweetheart, does a bear go poop in the woods?" The last cowboy laughed.

"I guess some do, the ones that don't live in outhouses," Mariana laughed and reached for his hand. They stood up together and walked outside. It had stopped snowing and the winter sun had completely broken through the fat, gray clouds, but it was still cold, bitter cold. For a brief instant, Mariana thought one of the clouds looked just like her son Sherman's misshapen head. But the cowboy's arm around her waist made her forget everything except the deep dryness of her throat and the deep dryness of her soul.

"We're gonna have us a good time," she said.

The old White man giggled and squeezed her tighter.

"You betcha," he said.

"You got that right," she answered and asked for another cigarette. She wanted to look at that wad of bills one more time. Something about it gave her a delirious shiver of hope.

Song of the Warrior

The reservation opened its arms and embraced springtime. Familiar with harsh winters, the people were used to gathering up the quickly thawing pieces of their lives and carrying on. Although winter always hit with the thoroughness of a fine-tooth comb, its touch was really more that of a gigantic rake. It plowed the earth and threw everything into confusion. In the spring, men often awoke in the arms of different wives. Entire families changed allegiances. Fence lines changed. Cars and children changed ownership and dogs, well, dogs remained the same.

Now, it was spring and the Indian universe was momentarily sweet, soft, and nurturing. After four months of nightmares, the artillery, the rockets, and the constant small arms fire in Teddy Two Bears' ears quieted and he cried without stopping for two days. It was late April, the time of the lover's flute, the time of rebirth and the time of new birth. He was back on his own land, and the White man's war over Middle Eastern oil was slowly becoming a distant, itchy memory.

Outside his parents' HUD house, random furry tremblings softened the morning. Rabbits scurried just beyond his front yard and in the near distance bucktoothed prairie dogs cavorted around their holes. Even farther away, Teddy saw an old coyote dressed in coveralls, strolling on his hind legs with a corncob pipe in his mouth.

Teddy stretched his lean, six-foot frame and sat up in bed. He rubbed the sleep from his eyes and stared through his bedroom window and smiled at the sight of a young doe on a nearby hillside. She was grazing, almost hidden by the shadows of the tall cottonwoods, which were just beginning to unfurl their waxen leaves.

Teddy smiled and got out of bed and hobbled around the room until he stood before a cracked mirror on the wall. He rubbed his short army haircut, popped a blackhead on his chin, and then blew a kiss at himself. He was still smiling when he walked down the hallway to the bathroom and took a shower. When he finished, he could hear his mother in the kitchen making coffee and frying bacon. His mother was singing an old Indian love song.

He went back to his bedroom and got dressed in some faded jeans and an old football jersey. The last item he put on was the pair of specially made shoes that allowed him to walk halfway normal. He was missing a third of his left foot. It had been exploded into hamburger by an Iraqi land mine buried beneath the blistering sands of Kuwait. The Iraqi land mine, like the shoes, had been American-made. Nevertheless, the shoes, which had been made for him during his stay in Fitzsimmons Hospital in Denver, gave him a walk that was not all that different from the way he'd walked before he went away to war.

Before he'd joined the army, he walked with a slight spring in his step. Before he'd shipped out, he walked like a virgin.

And when he came home, he still walked that way, although he had a slight hobble. Teddy was twenty years old, and his best friends were bound and determined to see him lose his cherry before he reached twenty-one. His birthday was two days away. On the reservation, it was unheard of these days for a man his age to be a virgin. Unless, of course, that man was gay. And Teddy was. But that was a secret even his closest childhood friends were unaware of.

Teddy did not act feminine, did not give longing glances to men, and did not give any indication whatsoever that he was a homosexual. In fact, he still dated girls, but he had absolutely no sexual interest in them. He never had, but now he felt like he had to prove himself.

He was a combat veteran and his best friends had bent over backwards, doing everything to make the returning hero feel like they all loved him. Now they were planning a birthday party, and they had hinted that he would get laid at it. This made Teddy uneasy. He'd never had sex with a woman, but he'd had a brief affair with a man, a short, blond air force captain he'd met during Desert Storm. It wasn't much of an affair. He and the captain had only gotten together secretly three times for three furtive rounds of mutual masturbation.

"We get caught we're fucked," the captain had said on each of the three occasions. "No more after this," he said at the last meeting.

The partying that night of his birthday started off slowly. Teddy and four of his high school buddies sat at White Clay Dam listening to crickets and drinking a case of beer. They sat on the hoods of their cars telling jokes and in the silence between the words, they ignored the noisy frogs and coyotes. A warm black blanket sprinkled with sharp, sparkling stars covered the Indian earth. They were young and just beginning to have a good time. Later they planned to go over to Gus

Winters' house out in the country for Teddy's "birthday surprise."

Gus had been Teddy's best friend in high school, but in the
past two years the two had grown some distance between them.
Sometimes Teddy wondered if Gus suspected that Teddy had
gay blood coursing through his veins. Gus sat next to him at
the dam and seemed intent on opening Teddy's beers as quickly
as possible. In the flickering light of a small campfire they'd
built, Teddy stole a sidelong glance at his friend and felt a
slight twinge of sadness.

"*Kola,*" Teddy said.

"*Kola,*" Gus answered.

Gus Winters was a short man, pimpled, muscular, and very
light-skinned for an Indian. He had pale blue eyes and had a
series of homemade tattoos running up both his arms. He
had already started to drink much too heavily for his young
age. His main goal in life was to win some money on the
rodeo circuit, and this seemed natural since he had been
around horses and cows all his life. Gus was an Indian cowboy.

"Let's head on out to my crib," Gus told the crowd. "It ain't
every day my parents and sister are spending the night in
Rapid City. We got some serious partying to do and Teddy,
well, Teddy's got some serious porking to do."

"Hahhhh," came a chorus of laughter.

"Teddy, do you know any woman name of Mariana Two
Knives?" asked Denny Lance. It looked like he was trying to
strangle a giggle from coming out.

"Naw, I don't think so—"

"She's a knob gobbler," Gus piped in.

"What the hell's a knob gobbler?" Teddy asked. He had never
heard the term before and it puzzled him.

"You don't know?" Denny giggled.

"She'll gobble your knob," Gus hooted.

"She's kind of a hobgoblin, too," Gary Red Horse laughed.
Then everyone except Teddy began to laugh uncontrollably.

"Hobgoblin, hahh," said Gus and then started making a ghostly sound, "Ooooohhhhhoooo. Hobgoblin knob gobbler. Oooooohhhhhooo."

Then everyone, Teddy included, though he didn't exactly know why, started making the same spooky sound. "Ooooohhhhhooooo."

"Let's ride, you knob gobblers," Gus said and stood up. "We're gonna get Rambo here some prime whisker biscuit."

Teddy and his four friends then chortled in unison. Beneath his exterior composure, Teddy squirmed. It was out in the open now. They did have a woman waiting at the Winters' place. And before he knew it, the young men were driving in a convoy of two cars to the site of the virgin sacrifice. His heart began to beat faster, his palms began to sweat, and a bitter anger began to rise.

Teddy rode with Gus and Gary Red Horse. Elmer Rodriguez and Denny Lance followed in another car behind them. Elmer and Denny had been the quarterback and center on the high school football team, and they were best buddies, although often the butt of the jokes of their other friends.

"Elmer bent over in front of Denny so much that they fell in love," Gus once teased, but Teddy knew for a fact that neither one had the slightest hint of homosexuality. Denny and Elmer were just close friends, almost like brothers. In fact, all five were best friends, and truly like brothers, although now Teddy could feel himself growing away from their well-cultivated immaturity. The reservation was a place where many men never really seemed able to mature fully.

Teddy wondered what his friends would really say if they ever found out that he was a knob gobbler too. They'd have spastic diarrhea of the brain. They'd drop him like a hot potato and maybe kick his ass for good measure. Like many Rez guys, they would go through their whole lives without really growing up and accepting any individual responsibility at all. Teddy knew how they were. He had known all of them since kindergarten. Their patterns were set for life.

Gary Red Horse, a two-hundred-fifty-pound fullblood, was slightly different from the rest of the crew. He was mostly serious, and always extremely kind to children and old people. He wore thick glasses and often dropped hints of wanting to enter the priesthood. He had been a straight-A student in high school, and his only flaw was that once a month or so he went on a hellacious drunk and blacked out. He had once told Teddy how much this troubled him. "So quit drinking," Teddy had told him. Gary kept on drinking and feeling guilty.

When they got to the Winters' place, Teddy surveyed the scene and tried to control his nerves. Dogs barked eerily as the two vehicles parked in front of the main house. The one-story prefab house was surrounded by nearby corrals and all the lights inside seemed to be on. The drapes over the picture window in the living room were open and Teddy could see someone sitting in the living room watching television. It was a woman, an Indian woman, and she was wearing a white blouse and black jeans.

The boys burst through the front door dragging Teddy with them. In a burst of guffaws, they grabbed the woman off the couch and pushed her toward Teddy. Before Teddy could open his mouth, he butted foreheads with the woman and they both screeched in pain.

"Damn, why don't you guys grow up?" the woman squealed.

"Sorry," said Teddy and looked closer at the person he'd just collided with. She wasn't very attractive, was a few years older than him and looked rugged from years of hard drinking. Something about her was vaguely familiar.

"This here's Mariana Two Knives," Gus blurted out and took her hand and placed it in Teddy's. Teddy stared hard at her and finally figured out he had known her in grade school. She'd been a couple years ahead of him, but he'd never really known her well at all.

"Well," Mariana said.

"Well, what?" Teddy replied, just starting to feel the pulsing swirl effect of the beers on his brain.

"You ain't related to me, are you?" she asked.

"Not that I know of," he said.

"Well," she said.

"Spit it out," he said, slightly exasperated.

"These guys hired me to get your cherry. That's what."

"Ah, man," Teddy said and rubbed his forehead.

"You're a virgin, right?" Mariana asked. "Tell me. It's nothing to be shamed of."

Teddy became mute and forced his mind back to the day the land mine had blown up underneath him. It was a very dim memory. He did not want to be in this house with his friends and this strange woman. What kind of a woman would do the deed for money anyways? Prostitutes were unheard of on the reservation. Women might screw for wine or glory, but never for money. And she looked like a run-of-the-mill drunk. If he had to make love to a woman, he'd prefer one that didn't have such jagged edges and wasn't so close to butt-ugly.

"Sure, sure he is," Gus shouted. "Gobble his goblin now."

"You wanna go to the bedroom?" Mariana laughed and then coughed. "Come on, bro, I ain't got all night."

Then all four of Teddy's friends began their chorus: "The bedroom now, the bedroom now, the bedroom now, gobble-gobble."

"You heard them, let's go," she said.

Teddy had no choice. He allowed Mariana to take his hand and lead him to Gus's bedroom. Gus had installed a red lightbulb in the small lamp on his nightstand. The glowing redness made Teddy feel like he was descending into hell. Everything was softly red and fuzzy. He heard Mariana shut the door behind them, and he could hear her getting undressed. He felt his scrotum tighten up and his penis shrivel.

"Damn, take your clothes off. I ain't got all night," she said in a low whisper that had no hint of affection.

"I don't know if I'm in the mood," he said and did not move.

"Mood or not, we're going to get it on," she said. "Mood, hah. All you guys ever think of is getting laid anyways. Who are you trying to kid? Try it. You know you'll like it."

"I don't think I want to," Teddy said.

"What are you talking about, man? They already paid me."

"I don't want no wham-bam-thank-you-ma'am."

"Well, geez, boy. Just what do you want? You want some head then those guys gotta give me some more bread. Blow jobs cost extra and I don't like to do that, but I will. I don't swallow jizz."

"I only agreed to this because it's my birthday. I'm not really even a virgin. I've had sex before," he said. His voice was starting to slur. The beers he'd drunk rapidly were beginning to realign his brain cells.

"Yeah? You been with a woman before?" Mariana was now completely naked and running her hands over her droopy breasts.

"No, not exactly." He turned his eyes away from her nakedness and sat on the edge of the bed.

"Oh, geez, I see it now," she said. "I see it now, I see it now. You're gay, aren't you? You're a gay boy. My, my. A queer Skin."

Teddy did not answer. His stomach was starting to turn flip-flops. He looked at the ceiling, which was slowly starting to revolve. He knew he was drunk. Maybe he could do it. Maybe it wouldn't be too bad.

"Well, if you like men, you like men," she said. "Nothing much I can do about that, but I ain't giving the money back."

"I don't like men," he said weakly.

"I know guys like you. Whatever, like I say, I'm not giving you back the money."

"You don't have to," he said. "Keep it. It's okay."

"And just what are we supposed to tell your buddies out there?" Mariana said and lit a cigarette in the red-flushed darkness. "That you don't wanna do it because you're a *winkte*?"

"Just say we did it," Teddy said lamely.

"That's gonna cost you an extra twenty," she said.

"What for?" Teddy demanded. "You didn't even have to do nothing. Those guys already paid you, right?"

"They did, but I need an extra twenty not to tell them you're a *winkte*. That seems a fair price to me."

"I ain't got twenty," he said and watched her begin to get dressed. "Why are you being a bitch to me? I never did anything to you." She slowly pulled on her jeans. She wasn't wearing panties.

"You give me twenty or I tell them. I bet you wouldn't like that one bit. Here they go and hire me for your birthday and you can't even do it because you like boys. What do you think they'd say?"

Teddy knew all hell would break loose if she told them. Drunk as he was, this was not the time to come out of the closet.

"I was just kidding," he said.

"Kidding? About what?"

"About not wanting to do it," he said. "I want to do it with you. I was just kidding. I want to screw you. I want you to be a knob gobbler."

"Knob gobbler? What the hell's that? Hey, kid, what's with you anyways? Are you drunk or just stupid? Make up your mind. You wanna do it, then let's do it. I sure thought you were queer the minute I seen you."

"Naw, I ain't," he said. "Get undressed again and lay on the bed. I gotta go get us a couple beers. How's that sound? A couple of ice-cold Buds would be nice, *ennut*?"

"Good idea," she said and pulled off her pants and lay naked on the bed. "Get me some Kleenex too."

Teddy walked naked out into the living room where his four friends from childhood were more subdued now, drinking beer and watching *Star Trek: The Next Generation* on the tube.

"Who's ready for sloppy seconds?" Teddy yelled. As a group, the Indian boys rose and ran drunkenly, gleefully toward the bedroom. Teddy sat down and stared at Captain Jean-Luc Picard of the *Enterprise*. Something about him reminded Teddy of another captain he had known. He thought warm thoughts of him as he heard Mariana Two Knives screaming, swearing, and kicking in the bedroom.

Raven Bombs the Screamer

Raven was famished, but nothing he fixed seemed to satisfy his appetite. He opened a can of pork and beans, heated them, and then doused them with Louisiana Hot Sauce. They tasted horrible, so he flushed them down the toilet. Then he popped two square frozen waffles into his square toaster, but when they were done he discovered he was out of maple syrup. He ended up eating a peanut butter and banana sandwich, which tasted gummy and bland. At least it was square. He missed Alicia's cooking. No, he missed Alicia, period, that silly, round Indian woman.

The television had become his only companion. Raven was sober and didn't have a single ruffled feather. He was thinking about going out and celebrating the second anniversary of his divorce from Alicia. He was getting bored with watching CNN's around-the-clock news. It was easy to overdose on the all-news channel. Things were always happening.

Frankly, Raven was tired of the entire civilized world. It was the day before the Fourth of July, a silly holiday invented by the White man. He pictured the entire population of America gathering around their mind control machines on Independence Day to watch a lone bottle rocket fizzle. An ad for an exercise video called *Buns of Steel* made him wince. He thought anyone who had Buns of Steel was more than likely to have rusty bloomers.

Raven was most tired of the poor humans who were ruining the country. He believed these uneducated hordes and their gangster ways were beyond hope and were turning the States into numerous Beiruts. It was clear to him that America was chockful of vile and violent people. This was no startling revelation. The bird world had known this for centuries. Many bird nations, like many Indian tribes, had been totally exterminated.

While waiting for the French cooking show *Cuisine Rapide* to come on, he tuned in to Rush Limbaugh. Raven had grown to like the chubby conservative commentator. He agreed with him and could clearly see how poverty and the broken American dream combined to form gangs of whites, browns, reds, and blacks, and even yellows! The gangs of humans had no dignity, no honor like the varied flocks of birds did. Raven realized that sometimes he thought just like a rich White man.

Raven longed for the days when the cold fear of Mother Russia was the glue that held the world together. The fear of atomic war was pure and honest. It was a clean, four-cornered fear. Maybe America needed a new Secret Police. A new constitutional amendment should read: "If you screw up, murder, rob, rape, and plunder, then forget any liberal wrist-slapping, you simply get your tallywhacker chopped off."

Here, now, in this country, in the tail end of the twentieth century, he knew that the humans lived the lie of democracy. The whole country was off-kilter. Here on the Indian reservation, once a month, the descendants of Crazy Horse lined up behind a semi-truck and collected free boxes of government cheese.

Crazy Horse was probably babbling in his grave. Everything in America was screwed up. Even the laws of the land were crooked. There was truly taxation without representation. The most famous defense attorney in America had gone on television the week before and said it is common practice for U.S. attorneys and most feds to manufacture evidence. The government was failing badly. Maybe it always had.

Raven tried to check his high blood pressure. Rush Limbaugh had elevated it, so he changed channels and saw reporters running after the president. Florid, semi-puffy Bill Clinton was jogging, sweating out his weekly collection of Big Macs and dodging questions about how we bombed the starving Somalis because they refused to clean their plates.

Raven had had enough. He switched off the tube and flew out the square window. He would find a human to defecate on. That would give him some solace. He winged his way to a tall cottonwood near the tribal administration building. The sun bounced off his black feathers and made him feel good. He was scanning the ground for a likely victim when he heard an unearthly screeching. It was a human, obviously three bricks short of a load. A screamer.

"Aiiiiiiyyyyeeeeeeyi," the screamer screamed.

"Amen, brother," Raven chortled.

Raven watched the screamer break free of the shadows and stare straight into the sun. Dancing upon the grill of shimmering sidewalks, the gangly fullblood in a grimy shirt and straw Stetson temporarily halted the quick migration of sleepwalking suits from one air-conditioned BIA dream to another with his mad mixture of biblical logarithms and recipes for Indian torment or triumph.

Although he was an A-1 screamer, he was scoffed at by some of the audience wilting in the twelve o'clock ninety-nine-degree heat.

"Poor thing, it can't be that bad," an old woman wearing a blue bandanna said in Indian.

"Lock the damn fool up," a tribal cop mumbled.

"Hey, cousin, give us a taste of what you're drinking," a wino whispered and nudged his buddy in the ribs.

"Must be on crack cocaine," some young boys with baggy pants and backwards ball caps said. "He's awesomely stoned."

Still others crawled back into the dark corners of their neatly trimmed minds and silently screamed at the mad release of unrecognized ghosts. The screamer heard them and smiled. Satisfied, he climbed onto a gaunt gray horse and loped back to report in to his bosses.

The regional sales office of Screamers International was located in that part of the reservation where cable television did not reach and where old people sat in outhouses contemplating a universe where everything sold had ninety-nine cents as its price. If any train tracks ran through the reservation, then that part where he went would definitely be on the wrong side of them.

Raven took off from the tall tree and gained altitude. Then he dove toward the earth in a black blur and gushed out a huge pile of crow crap that splattered the screamer directly in the face.

"That one's for the Gipper," Raven cackled.

"Aiiiiiyyeeeeeeeeeiiiiiiiiieeeeeekkkkk," the screamer screamed. He had manufactured one of the most vicious and most earth-shattering screams in the history of humankind. Raven laughed and flew off chortling "caw-caw" to the entire world, but he was not satisfied. What was the point of crapping on a crazy man? In fact, he was more depressed than ever and the main reason was because he'd heard on the Moccasin Telegraph that Alicia had found a new beau—and that she was planning to marry him.

He flew back to the cottonwood tree and stewed. Just the thought of some stinking human straddling and humping his ex-wife made his feathers shrivel. He would fly to Alicia's house and simply tell her not to marry him. He would fly back into her life as easily as he had flown out. He was a man, damn it, and she was just a woman.

He somersaulted into the air and beat his wings toward Alicia's house. She was working in her small garden, pulling weeds and watering her fledgling zucchini and tomatoes. He landed on a small, weathered wooden fence that surrounded the garden. Her garden was not normal. It was not square. It was round and surrounded by a round fence.

"Gardens should be square," he said and stared into her eyes. She did not show the slightest hint of fear.

"What are you doing here?" she asked.

"I still love you, Alicia," he said in what he thought was an extremely sincere voice.

"You mean you still wanna own me. You mean you still wanna terrorize me with verb abuse," she said.

"'Verbal,' you mean 'verbal.' Hey, look, I've changed," Raven said lamely and tried to scrinch his beak into a smile.

"Fat chance," she said and turned her back to him. "You still scare me so much I can't look you in the eyes. I used to be independent, free, and happy. You took all that from me."

"Alicia . . . if I did, I could give it back to you. I need you. I still love you, I do, damn it."

"You'll never change," she said and reached down to pull up a handful of ironweed from among her tomatoes.

"I'll change, I can change—"

"Forget it," she said. "You better make tracks. My new boyfriend is due back for lunch any minute now. And don't come back. We're through. We're ancient history."

Raven heard footsteps behind him. He turned his neck in a full circle and saw the screamer walking toward him. The screamer was carrying a double-barreled twelve-gauge shotgun.

"Not him, Alicia. You got to be kidding," Raven chortled. "That guy's a wacko, a nutcase."

"Well, it's true, he does scream a lot, but he doesn't scream at me," Alicia said. "You better go. He's the jealous type."

"You!" Raven cawed as the screamer approached.

"You! You birdshitter," the screamer screamed and fired. Flame and lead belched out of both round barrels.

"You filthy animal!" the screamer screamed.

"Missed me, you retard," Raven replied and raised his wings above his head to fly the hell out of there.

"You!" the screamer screamed and quickly reloaded and fired both barrels again.

Raven did not reply. Again, he was hurtling through a black sky, but this time he was unaware of it or anything else. The black sky easily absorbed the explosion of black bird feathers. Raven no longer existed.

"Darling," Alicia whispered to the screamer.

"Darling," the screamer screamed back.

Coyote in the City of Angels

It was a skanky summer day in Los Angeles. The sun beat down upon the garbage dumpsters and gave the unmoving air a bad case of rotten breath. The sidewalks baked, drawing moisture out of the mouths of every living thing. Up in Holly- wood, the dealmakers were looking for a live brain to suck ideas out of. Down in South Central and over in East L.A., the residents were going about their daily business of mur- dering each other.

On the downtown side of Pico-Union, Coyote had spent the entire morning searching for a lifesaving, cool drink of fire water. It had been over six months since he'd left the Great Plains and nearly a year since his wife had got bit by a squirrel with rabies and died. Even though he wasn't living with her at the time, her death propelled him toward seeking his own. He'd put his dogs in the care of Old Bear and hit the road, then the skids, and had rejoined the shadow soldiers in the Grand Army of Booze.

Coyote was a sorry sight to see. He'd developed a severe case of mange and not only had frequent shaking spells, but he smelled bad. He stank of disease and impending death. Day after day, he'd dragged his swollen paws over the scorched pavement, his tail dangling between his legs. Now staggering to a shabbier street, he saw a small blue building with winking neon signs that beckoned him. The bar was named The Shanty and was frequented by citified Indians and other denizens of the once-natural world.

Coyote's only thought was of cold liquid trickling down his parched throat and then up to pacify his fiery brain. Shaking, drawing up all his strength, he assumed as straight a posture as possible, put his right foot forward and entered the blue building. Stumbling in the darkness, he stubbed his toe on a chair. It hurt like hell, and he did a strange dance until the pain subsided. He felt like a fool until he found a stool and sat down, waiting for his eyes to adjust to the darkness.

"Whatcha want, Cuz?" asked a burly, dark-skinned human with a shaved head.

Coyote stared at the man. "Don't I know you?"

"I don't know. Do you?"

"I'm from South Dakota," Coyote said.

"No kiddin', what Rez? I'm from Rapid City, originally from Pine Ridge," the man said. "My name is Verdell Ten Bears. Got in a little trouble back home and headed out."

"Never heard of you," Coyote said with an apologetic shrug of his bony shoulders. "Sorry, I thought you looked familiar."

"All us savages look the same. Take my word on it. You don't know me from Shinola. I don't know that many coyotes anyways. The only coyotes I ever saw were those that got nailed by speeding UPS trucks or those in hunters' traps."

"Very funny," Coyote said and coughed to hide his disgust. He knew for a fact that when Indians disappeared into the steel and concrete canyons of cities they changed. They became hopeless, lost, or just like the White men. To him, urban Indians were the most pitiful of God's creatures, even more pitiful than the White man.

"So what is it? What can I do you for?" Ten Bears asked.

"A cool, cool drink," Coyote answered.

"A drink of what—"

"Gin and tonic's okay," Coyote said as he handed the man a handful of change that he had panhandled earlier. The shaved head brought him a large glass of cold, clear liquid with a slice of unhealthy lime floating atop it. Coyote lifted the glass to his lips and then screamed. There was a monster in the glass! He poured out the contents onto the floor and asked the man for another.

"It's your money, dude," the man said and brought Coyote another large tumbler of the liquid.

Again, Coyote raised the glass to his lips, but again he saw the monster on the surface of the clear liquid.

"Arrrggghhh-aroooo," Coyote screamed. "What is this funky creature in my drink? What the hell is going on here? What the hell is this? Psychedelic gin?"

The large, scary-looking bartender ignored him. The human named Ten Bears acted like this was an everyday occurrence. Coyote decided to take action. He bared his teeth and raised the glass to his lips. He would show the monster how ferocious he was and it would run. It didn't, though. Coyote looked into the glass and cringed. Inside, on the surface of the liquid, a dark, hairy, repulsive monster stared back with bared teeth. Coyote drew back in terror. Coyote slapped his face to try to regain a grasp around reality's neck. He hoped this monster in his drink wasn't a prelude to the shimmering d.t.'s.

He sat on his haunches and took a deep breath. Maybe the monster would leave of its own accord. It certainly was one of the ugliest beasts he'd ever seen in his life. After a few minutes, Coyote leaned forward and looked into the glass. The monster was still there. Coyote panicked and ran out of the blue building, forgetting his deep thirst. But, after a few desperately alcoholic minutes in the heat, he recalled that there was yet another blue building on the same block.

Although he was tired, dirty, and half-cooked from the heat, Coyote walked in the direction of the second blue building. He would find a cool drink there. His thirst was what propelled each step. All during the journey down the never-ending block, the face of the monster from the other building danced in his mind.

"That was one skanky-lookin' bugmugger," Coyote whispered to no one in particular. "One ugly hunk of head cheese."

The sun was beginning to set, and still there was no relief from the heat. Coyote could walk no farther and fell asleep in a cool alleyway behind a large green dumpster. He was so exhausted that he slept through the whole night and awoke the next morning when the sun was high in the sky.

Tired and disoriented but more thirsty than he had ever been in his life, he decided to go back to the first blue building. His thirst was now greater than his fear of the monster in the glass. His throat was on fire as he entered the building. He would kill anything that stood between him and the lifeblood of liquor.

"Oh, you again," said the dark, muscular man with no head hair as he wiped down the cigarette-scarred bar. Coyote nodded and ordered a large drink.

"Same as before?" Ten Bears asked.

"Same and hurry," Coyote rasped.

"Here you go," the bartender said as he handed Coyote the gin and tonic. Before looking into the glass, Coyote handed it to another human, a grizzled old Mexican sitting at the bar. This Mexican, a former assistant organizer in the United Farm Workers, took the glass and half drained it. He burped and nodded at Coyote, but Coyote grabbed the glass back and prepared to drink the remaining half.

"*Gracias,*" the old man muttered.

"If this old Pancho Villa can drink it safely, then the monster must have gone," Coyote mumbled low and raised the glass to his lips. He closed his eyes and took a deep, refreshing gulp. The liquid was pure heaven, and his aching bones and flaming soul felt instantly relieved. He poured the remaining liquid down his dry, sandy gullet.

"Salvation," he shouted at the Indian named Ten Bears.

"That mean you want another?"

"Yes, damn rights, get me another," he yelled at the bartender. When the fresh drink arrived, he noticed to his great dismay that the monster had reappeared. He slammed the glass down in fear and disgust. The vibrating glass caused ripples on the surface of the gin and the monster disappeared. Coyote thought this strange and stared until the liquid was calm again. And when the booze had stopped vibrating, the hideous creature was back on the surface again.

Coyote took his paw, placed a claw in the liquid and stirred it. Again, the monster vanished. Coyote then realized that the ghastly creature was his own reflection.

"For crying out loud," he roared. "Hah-hah-hooooo." He laughed so loud that everyone in the bar stared at him. Coyote giggled and ordered another drink. He had a pocket full of change from panhandling and nothing now stood between him and blissful intoxication.

"For a while there, I thought I might be seeing snakes crawl up the walls. For one brief second, I actually contemplated joining up with those AA whiny asses," he told the bartender.

"AA sucks a big one," Ten Bears shouted.

"Yo, screw AA and the horse it rode in on," Coyote repeated.

"You got that," Verdell Ten Bears said and shrugged, then

glared and walked away. He was a practicing drunk and had been for years. Even the thought of going to AA made him want to kick ass on somebody, anybody.

For a brief moment, Coyote considered slamming Ten Bears in the back of the head with his glass. The monster was now inside him and he felt the power of a god. He was sick of mankind.

"The hell with this city," he said to no one in particular. But outside, thousands of Blacks and Chicanos had somehow heard him. They nodded in assent at the new voice of God and began to burn down the "City of Angels."

Edwin's Letter
About *A Man Called Horse*

Edwin Takes The Bow had been drinking heavy ever since he found out that Abner Red Eagle had been voted out of office. Abner had been tribal chairman for the past two years, and Edwin was his assistant press relations officer. What that meant was that Edwin got the thankless job of answering letters written to the chairman by goofballs all over America who had no real contact with Indian people but wanted to know so much more.

"Americans are hungry for Indian lore as long as they never have to smell a real live Indian," Edwin told the secretary when she handed him a stack of letters. In two more weeks, the new administration would take over the reins of control. Because he was so sick of his job and somewhat relieved at the same time, Edwin had been drinking heavy.

He was also sick of his first cousin Abner. Edwin had been to college and Abner had not. Because of this, Edwin viewed his cousin as little more than just another dumb Skin. Abner was short and fat, had a flattop haircut and wore glasses, and Edwin suspected that Abner was diddling his wife on the side. If there ever was a sneaky Indian who spoke out of both sides of his mouth, Edwin knew it was Abner Red Eagle.

Edwin was tall and lean and wore braids, and he was hungover when he reported to work that Monday. He was dressed casually. Jeans and knit polo shirt and Nikes. No sense in playing the white shirt and tie game anymore. The people had spoken. They had voted Abner Red Eagle out of office because he was an incompetent womanizer. Edwin sat at his desk at ten past nine and computed that it would be two hours and forty-five minutes before he could go home for lunch and for some hair of the dog.

Edwin was on the phone to his soon-to-be-ex wife, who was bitching about the disposal of various community property, when one of the chairman's secretaries dropped yet another pile of already opened mail on his desk. He watched her tight little butt wiggle away. She was wearing a short blue satin skirt and you could see the outline of her panties beneath it.

Chairman Red Eagle had three secretaries and once had boasted to Edwin that he had had them all at once one night at a BIA conference in Aberdeen. The mere thought of sex made Edwin's stomach tumble. He said a silent prayer that his hangover would vanish, and then he hung up on his wife before she had finished her tirade. This time she'd wanted to know if he was in possession of two coffee cups from the plate set her aunt had given them as a wedding gift.

Edwin rubbed his eyes and his hand automatically went to the mail pile. More letters to answer. Always answer the letters was the policy. You never can tell when a nice prompt reply might bring the tribe (meaning Abner Red Eagle) some donation from some rich nitwit who thought Indians were a noble lot.

Edwin sliced open the first envelope with a Swiss Army knife that he kept on his desk for use as a letter opener. The letter was addressed to the "Chief of the Siouxs." That made Edwin wince. It was from a third grade class in West Lafayette, Indiana. Edwin began to read and roll his eyes at the same time.

Room 3-B
Plainview Elementary School
West Lafayette, IN

Dear Chief of the Siouxs,
    We would like some information on the movie *A Man Called Horse*. The star was named John Morgan. He was an English and lived among you Siouxs. They made him chief and gave him the name Yellow Hand. Did he have a son name of Kowda? Did his son have an Indian girl named Red Wing Crow? Did he have a friend name of Elk Woman? Did his son stay with the Siouxs the rest of his life? Write us back and let us know if this story is true.

    P.S. Do you still live in teepees? And where do you keep your buffalos now?
                              From Miss LaVierre's Third Grade Class
                              West Lafayette, Indiana

Edwin squinted and for an instant debated tossing the letter into the circular file. *Four years of college*, he thought, *and now I sit and answer horseshit like this.*
    "Two more weeks," he said to no one in particular and scratched his head. He lit a cigarette and rolled a sheet of bond paper with tribal letterhead into his IBM Actionwriter.

My Dear Miss Brassiere:
    Please tell your rug rats that the story just might be true. Some dude in the Pejuta Haka district of this reservation told me that a man named Horse did come to live among us wild-ass Sioux during the late '60s.

This dude's full name was Larry Horse Pahtootey. Although he lived among us Sioux, he had two brothers who lived with other tribes. Their names were Moe and Curly, and all three brothers were members of a nearly extinct tribe called WASP liberals. Their avowed goal in life was to save the Indians from themselves.

Larry Horse Pahtootey came to the land of the Sioux in the guise of a VISTA worker. He came to save our poor, noble, and wretched red men from our "plight." He worked long hours, grew long hair, and lived just like us natives. He ate government cheese and occasionally sprang for a pint of cheap wine, which he would share with the winos. He even wrote long letters home detailing the good work he was doing here.

Of course, nothing he ever did amounted to a hill of beans. What he was really doing was escaping the bland and inhuman quality of the "great society" he had been born into. He was looking for his soul because as you know, so many of you *wasicus* are born without one. He saw that many Indian people were living a lifestyle that made him envious. Some of the people he worked for didn't give a damn about anything, including themselves, but he was trying to help them anyway.

This man named Horse wanted to be an Indian more than anything. It just wasn't fair, he thought, that Indianness was wasted on Indians who did not appreciate their noble status. He learned the basics of Sioux linguistics, he learned to brain-tan hides, and he learned to make tripe soup. He even fell in love with and married a fullblood Indian woman. She soon left him, so his next step was to adopt some Indian kids.

When these kids got into trouble, he disciplined them the way he had been disciplined. He spared the rod. The kids became such raise-hells that the state Department of

Social Services came in and took them away from Larry. The kids ended up worse off than they had been before Larry intervened. These kids had "state penitentiary" tattooed across their future.

Finally, Larry Horse Pahtootey gave up on trying to save the Indian people from themselves. He packed his bags and headed home. Today he lives in the suburbs in Connecticut. He commutes daily to New York City where he owns a sweatshop that employs illegal aliens from the land of bananas. He is trying to learn to talk Spanish.

His brother, Moe Horse Pahtootey, lived among the Navajo near Window Rock, Arizona. Moe was a self-styled educator. He had learned so many of the occult methods of education (including Montessori and "Whole Language") that he was able to secure a teaching position at Navajo Community College.

"I believe in indigenous tribal peoples," he told them after they hired him. "I want to walk the way of beauty," he said. Had he said that before he was hired, they probably would have tossed him out on his ear. They were astonished when he told them he would work for half the salary they offered because he felt the Navajo were "his people too."

"Your name ain't Hillerman?" they asked him.

Moe began to grow his hair long and then rolled it into a traditional Navajo bun. He learned to say *ya ta hey*. He shook hands with everyone he saw and solemnly said, "*Ya ta hey, hosteen.*" He organized a canned food drive with his White colleagues at the college. He was a formidably good organizer.

"He really cares about Indian people," his colleagues would tell each other.

"Who is this *bilagáana* nutbag?" the Navajo Indians would whisper among themselves.

As Moe's hair grew longer than any Navajo's, he began to find a new freedom. This showed in the way he ran his classes. He told all the students that they would be given automatic A's regardless of how they did in their coursework. "Competition is not the Indian way," he would tell them.

"Right on, bro," his students would answer and giggle behind his back.

Soon the students quit coming to his classes altogether. When he was questioned by tribal administrators as to what the hell he was doing in his classrooms, Moe defended his theories.

"It's an open classroom and people learn more when they're free," he said. "Compulsion is anti-learning," he told them.

When the administrators pointed out that they were paying him to teach, Moe rebelled. He went among those elders whose hands he'd shaken and to whom he'd given canned food.

"Brothers, I want to organize a protest march," he told them. "These tribal bureaucrats aren't acting in the Indian way. They don't know anything about education. I feel like I am one of you. I feel like I am Dineh."

None of the people would march for him or with him. The old ones thought he was loco. The younger ones, the very students who would no longer come to his classes, called him a "wannabe." Soon, the college had no option but to terminate him.

Single-handedly, for two days, he stood in front of the college administration building carrying a homemade sign protesting his firing. On the third day the tribal police hauled him away and tossed him into the tribal drunk tank.

"Brothers, *ya ta hey*," he greeted the dozens of stinky winos and bootleggers in the holding cell. They grunted back at him and within an hour beat the holy vinegar out of him.

And two big Mexicans had pulled his pants down and bent him over and, well . . .

When he was eventually released, Moe packed his bags and flew to the West Coast. Today, he owns a very successful used-car dealership in Northern California. And he could care less if he ever saw a real live redskinned Indian again.

The third brother was Curly Horse Pahtootey. He was an artist who had left home in the late '60s and hitchhiked to the Pyramid Lake Paiute Reservation in Nevada. All he took with him was his paintbrushes, his checkbook, and several extra T-shirts. He didn't wear underwear. It was the '60s way.

Of the three Horse Pahtootey brothers, Curly was the darkest. He moved into an abandoned farmhouse near the community of Wadsworth. He too grew his hair long and remained fairly anonymous until he had painted a large collection of stylized landscapes of the local area.

Curly actually told people on the Rez he was a Cherokee from Oklahoma.

"If I was a damn Cherokee, I sure wouldn't tell nobody," several Paiutes told him. Every Indian in America knew the Cherokees let anyone join up with that perplexing, ragtag mob they called a tribe.

Curly prospered. His art began to sell like hotcakes and the Nevada State Council on the Arts called him one of the finest native artists in the region. He began to date a Shoshone woman from Reno.

Curly built a sweat lodge behind his house and began to hold sweat ceremonies for White people, who would pay big bucks for such an exotic event. Curly began to tell people he was a pipeholder.

"This is the sacred pipe," he said to the local Indians as he proudly showed them a Sioux pipe that had real eagle feathers dangling from the stem. The Paiutes laughed at him. The Paiutes didn't put much stock in the "pipe religion," as it was more of a Plains Indian thing.

"What do you expect from a Cherokee?" they would ask and then roar with laughter. They would laugh and laugh and say things like "Cherokees ain't shit," and "Ain't Cher a Cherokee?"

Curly began to make the newspapers regularly with his art shows, sweats, and his teaching of the "Good Red Road."

"We Amerinds must all return to the good red road," he said on a local television show. "The ancestor spirits demand the old ways. The ancestor spirits still guide us."

One day after he received an appointment to teach art at the University of Nevada, a newspaper reporter for the *Nevada State Journal* in Reno called the Cherokee Tribe of Oklahoma to get some background on the illustrious artist.

"We ain't got him on the rolls," the Cherokee tribal enrollment officer told the reporter. "However, that don't mean he ain't a Cherokee," the officer added. "Our people are scattered all over the place."

When asked about this, Curly said, "I'm Indian because I am Indian. Being Indian has nothing to do with blood quantum—it's a matter of the spirit. I am a pipeholder. I always walk in balance. Whatever I do, I do as a warrior for my people. I will always walk in a sacred manner upon the sacred turtle's back."

The Paiutes didn't see it that way and did not buy his sacred turtle bullpoop. Therefore, it came to pass that one starry night Curly's house mysteriously burned down to the ground, consuming his sweat lodge and all his artwork. Curly was moved to copious tears. While watching the conflagration of his invented world, he had wet his pants.

The next night his car mysteriously exploded. The day after his car went boom, he drove to Reno and flew out on the first flight to Denver.

As far as we can tell, he now operates a successful leather shop there that caters strictly to the S&M trade. Curly wears a crew cut and dates only White truck drivers.

And so my Dear Ms. Brassiere, I hope this missive answers your students' questions about *A Man Called Horse.* Should you have further inquiries please refer them to the Horse Pahtootey brothers themselves. I suspect that they're listed in the phone books of whatever particular neighborhood of the Twilight Zone they now inhabit. None of them are now here in the land of us Siouxs.

Edwin reread the letter quickly and smiled. His hangover was beginning to dissipate. It was five minutes before noon. He stood up and visualized the ice-cold cans of Budweiser in his refrigerator. They'd taste good, he thought, and once this job ended, he'd quit the sauce.

Down the long hallway of the Tribal Administration Building, Edwin spotted Abner openly flirting with his secretaries. Edwin frowned and then he smiled deep down in his soul. He inserted the last sheet of his letter into the typewriter and completed his official act of correspondence by adding a final flourish:

P.S. And yeah, baby, we still got tipis. I'd like to get you in one and pull down your smooth, White-woman panties. As far as our buffalo, well, I guess they shuffled off. Please call me if you need to know more.

Savagely yours,
Abner Red Eagle
Tribal Chairman

Eagles Above Mean Good Luck?

The newly opened leaves of the elms chatter-danced together, proud of their perfect sheen. The morning breeze lifted the sexual aromas of spring through Teddy Two Bears' open window and woke him. It was the day after his twenty-first birthday. The night before, his friends had tried to help him lose his virginity by hooking him up with Mariana Two Knives. Teddy was still a virgin, at least with women, but his friends believed differently now. They truly believed he'd been the engine of the train they'd pulled on Mariana.

He could hear his mother brewing a pot of coffee and frying bacon and eggs in the kitchen. She would pour the leftover grease into a coffee can and later that evening when Teddy fed his three dogs, he would mix some of the grease into the dry dog food. Teddy vaguely recalled his father mixing their food that same way in those hazy childhood days before his father shipped off for Vietnam, where he died in the Tet Offensive.

"*Hoksila,* get up," his mother yelled at him. For an instant, a vision of his mother's face crossed his mind. He tried to imagine the expression on her face the day he would tell her he was gay. That was something he didn't really want to think about. He forced her face out of his mind.

"Okay, Ma," he shouted back as he reached down into his shorts to grasp his trout. Lately he had taken to masturbating to the vision of the blond air force captain he'd had a fling with during Desert Storm.

"Hurry up, boy, breakfast is getting cold," she said.

He rose moist from bed and began to get dressed in new Levi's and a western shirt. This was the day that his family was hosting a "welcome home" barbecue for him, and they'd invited relatives and friends from near and far. They had gotten a young buffalo from the tribe and had quartered it for the huge barbecue pit made of old oil drums cut lengthwise.

In his bedroom, he glanced occasionally at *Good Morning, America.* There upon the small portable television screen were the stone faces of Mount Rushmore. Incredibly, someone had splashed red paint all over George Washington's face. Arabs were suspected. He laughed and closed his eyes and said a brief prayer of thanks for the illusion God had allowed him to perform last night. The stigma of virginity had been erased and now he could concentrate and worry about more important things.

He took a deep breath and lit a cigarette. He heard the telephone ringing out in the living room. He listened to his mother answer it and then yell for him to come to the phone.

"It's a girl," she said proudly. "Says you know her and her name is Mary. A new girlfriend?"

Teddy didn't answer his mother. He simply smiled dutifully and picked up the receiver. Off the top of his head he could not recall knowing any girl named Mary.

"Hello," he said. "This is Teddy."

Silence.

"This is Teddy—"

"Teddy, the knob gobbler, right? Was that your mom who answered the phone? Wouldn't she like to know about you?" It was Mariana Two Knives. His stomach did a flip-flop and his heart fluttered. He felt afraid and strangely excited at the same time. *What the hell did she want and how had she gotten his phone number anyways?*

"How come you're calling—"

"Guess," she interrupted.

"How should I—"

"You assholes think you're so damn smart, don't you?" Teddy recoiled like he'd just come face to face with a ghastly living nightmare. He took a deep breath and scanned the room to make sure his mother had left.

"What do you want?" he said in a low voice, making sure his mother's keen ears could not hear what he was saying. "Why are you calling me? I didn't do anything to you, did I?"

"No, you didn't, you little queerboy, but your friends sure did. They pulled a gang bang on me and I didn't want it. I don't know what you call it, but I call it rape. And that Gus Winters kept slapping the hell out of me. He gave me a black eye."

"Ah, come off it," he said. "You were naked in bed. You wanted it. Right? Am I right or what? And besides, they gave you money."

"Yeah, I wanted it, but from you, not them. They paid me to have sex with you and I would have, but you turned out to be a homo. And I think you told those guys to come in and rape me."

"No, I didn't, why should—"

"You're one sick little *winkte*."

"Oh, come off it, Mariana. You don't even know me or anything about me. Why are you saying that?"

"I heard them boys last night talking about going to your family cookout today. What if I just show up and go up to your family and tell them you got a thing for having sex with men? How would you like that? Yeah, I might just tell them you're a cocksucker."

"What's your problem? Are you crazy or what? I never did anything to you. Why you messing with me?"

"Listen and listen good. I already told you once I think you told those guys to come in and rape me. I'm gonna make all of you pay, one way or another."

"Whaddya mean?" Teddy was slowly beginning to get exasperated with Mariana. Moreover, he was beginning to detest her, much like he would detest a pesky fly that kept landing on his nose while he was trying to sleep.

"I want a hundred bucks from each—"

"Hundred bucks! Dream on."

"I want a hundred bucks from each of you turdheads. And if you don't do it today, well then I make an appearance at your barbecue and that should be quite a scene, let me tell you. And if that don't work, well I guess I can always go to the cops."

"You'd put me in jail? For nothing?"

"You got that right, boy. Though maybe you'd like to spend some time at the state pen with all those Long Dong Silvers."

"Meet me out by the old powwow grounds in half an hour," he said. "I'll be there with the money."

"You're not there, I start talking," she said.

"I said I'd be there. See you."

"I thought so," she said and hung up. And as soon as he put down the receiver, the phone rang again. It was his aunt Theda calling to say she was making several gallons of potato salad and she needed some large containers. Teddy told her he'd get some from his mom and drop them off at her house shortly.

"Aunt Theda called and said her potato salad was almost

ready," he said. "She needs some containers. Said you had some large plastic buckets with lids. And to bring them over."

"Yeah, okay," his mother said. "So who was the other call? You got a new girlfriend you ain't telling me about?"

"No girlfriend. Just a girl I know. I'll run those buckets over to Aunt Theda's place now and I gotta stop in town for a little while before the barbecue. Okay if I take your car, Mom?"

"So who's Mary?"

"Just a girl I know . . ."

"Just a girl, huh? Well, don't be late for your dinner. We're starting out around one-thirty. All your friends and family want to see the returning war hero. Don't you dare be late. See you."

"I ain't no hero. See you."

Then the phone rang again. His mother answered it again and it was Mariana again. Teddy's face turned crimson and he had the metallic taste of fear in his mouth. He picked up the phone with a shaking hand. She wanted him to bring a six-pack of beer along with the money and make sure it was Budweiser. He said okay and hung up quickly. She was a seriously sick bitch, he thought.

"That your girlfriend again?" his mother teased.

"I don't have a girlfriend," he replied curtly and grabbed the car keys off a hook in the kitchen and strode briskly out the door.

"Get those two buckets in the shed," his mother shouted after him. "And tell Theda she better give them a good rinsing-out before she uses them. We ain't used them since last summer's big powwow."

"Okay, I'll be back in a little while," Teddy said over his shoulder. What should have been a day of joy and honor for him was rapidly turning into a nightmare. He got the buckets and loaded them into the trunk of his mother's dented '84 Ford Escort. His three dogs happily pounced on him and licked at him. They angered him. He kicked at the largest one, a black Lab, and missed. His stomach sank. Not once in his entire life had he ever done the smallest cruelty to his dogs.

"Get the hell back into your own world," he yelled at them and drove off, squealing the tires on his mom's car and leaving a large cloud of dust. For an instant, looking in the rearview mirror, he thought the cloud of dust might be following him. Bad spirits were in the air.

He dropped the plastic buckets at his aunt Theda's and then sped off to meet the madwoman Mariana. He stopped along the way at a bootlegger's and bought a six-pack of cold Budweiser at double the going rate. For a fleeting moment, he had a lovesick vision of the face of the air force captain who had briefly been his friend, confidant, and first lover. The recollection of his deep-blue eyes and blond hair calmed Teddy somewhat. He slowed the car down and sighed.

The powwow grounds were about half a mile from the center of town and were situated in a large stand of cottonwoods, which were themselves surrounded on all sides by clumps of wild cherry. When he pulled up in his mom's car, he expected to be alone, but Mariana was already waiting. He looked closely at her. She was disheveled and was wearing the same outfit she'd had on the night before. Yes, she *did* have a black eye. Maybe Gus *had* gotten a little rough with her. *Screw her!* She did look like some kind of damn hobgoblin. He shook his head in exasperation and contempt and got out of the car.

"About time," she said. "You got the beer?"

"I don't like the idea of you calling my house anyways," he said and dropped the six-pack of Budweiser onto the dusty ground near her feet. For an instant he wished he had the mental power to make the pop-tops open and shower this wino woman with beer foam.

"Hey, you'll shake them up," she yelled and reached down

quickly and snapped one can out of the plastic ring that bound it to the rest. She opened it and took a long drink.

"Tastes good," she said. "Want one?"

"I'm not here to socialize with you," Teddy said, unable to conceal his sarcasm any longer.

"Don't pout now," she said.

"Don't pout. Listen, for Christ's sake, you're blackmailing me. That's a felony."

"Blackmailing, hah! You wanna talk about crime, let's talk about rape. I'd say that's a little more serious, right?"

"I didn't rape you, and you know it."

"Well, every single one of your friends did. What the hell's the difference? If I say you did, you did. Or should we just go to the cops and get this settled?"

"Listen, Mariana. I ain't got no hundred bucks. I just got back from the military. I was in Desert Storm. In a couple weeks I will have some more pay coming in at the end of the month, but right now I'm broke. I ain't got an extra hundred. That's the truth."

"Okay, fine," she said and turned her back. "That's just fine, but I wonder what your parents are gonna say when I show up today and start telling them all how you're someone who just loves to take it up the butt."

A sharp pain shot from Teddy's neck all the way to the top of his head. "I can get the money," he said and noticed that his breathing was shallow and sweat was beading on his forehead.

"When?"

"Right now, damn it. Get in the car. We'll drive to Sioux Nation Shopping Center. I'll cash a check there."

"But I thought you were broke?"

"Get in the damn car."

"Well, that was easy," she said as she slid onto the front seat. "You're such a little queer," she said and reached over to muss his hair.

"Stop that, you scuzzy bitch," Teddy yelled and slapped at her face and missed. He had punched down on the gas pedal at the same instant. Mariana screamed and opened the car door and jumped before Teddy could react. The car was only moving about twenty-five miles an hour, but she hit the dirt and tumbled half a dozen times. His mind formed a short, instantaneous prayer.

"Jesus, oh Christ!" he screamed and slammed on the brakes. He jumped out of the car and ran back to where she lay. A million thoughts danced through his mind. He glanced at the shade arbors and briefly had a vision of the time he was ten years old and had won first place in the fancy-dance contest. He had won three hundred dollars and had bought a brand-new bike with his winnings. A ten-speed Schwinn.

"What the hell's the matter with you?" he said as he reached the place where Mariana lay in the dirt. "Are you crazy or what? Get up, god damn it. Get up now!"

Mariana did not move. Her face was covered with dust and her eyes were glazed. Her neck was clearly broken and her head pointed at a very odd angle. Teddy reached down, grabbed her wrist, and felt for a pulse. There was none. The sacred life spirit had left Mariana Two Knives. And the returning war hero had been the cause of her death.

"God help me," he mumbled and backed away from her still-warm body. His heart was beating like a war drum and tears were forming at the corners of his eyes. Nothing so horrible had ever happened in his life. Even the combat injury to his foot was minor compared to the predicament he now found himself in. "Dear God in heaven help me," he whimpered.

He didn't know what to do, so he forced himself to breathe deeply. After a minute of accelerated oxygenation, he convinced himself that he hadn't killed her. Damn, the crazy woman had jumped. He didn't push her. And they hadn't even been going fast enough to snap her neck. How the hell had that freak accident happened? It had happened in a flash before he knew it, just like the land mine that had blown up his foot in the Gulf. A flash, a horrible flash.

Sometimes life had grabbed him by the hand and led him into situations he did not want to be in. Sometimes he felt like a victim. He *was* a victim. He hadn't planned on losing his foot or on being of assistance in Mariana's death. Sometimes Teddy felt like he was cursed. He surely felt cursed by his desire for other men. That had been the cause of everything—he should have been a man and just diddled Mariana the night before and none of this would have happened.

"Damn you, damn you," he whispered through his clenched teeth at the young woman's corpse on the ground.

Teddy lifted her up and carried her to the car. He drove twenty yards away to a large clump of wild cherry and dumped her there. He looked around to make sure no one was watching, and he covered her completely with some dead branches.

Then he took a fallen cottonwood branch that still had leaves and dragged it over all the tire tracks he'd made near the powwow grounds. Satisfied, he stood up and walked backwards to the car, erasing any footprints his government shoes had made. For some reason, his limp had become more pronounced.

He got to the Ford and stood momentarily in the bright sunlight and saw two eagles floating through the blue sky.

Eagles were usually a good omen for Indians, but not today. He had to tell someone what had happened, but he knew if he told anybody, his whole life would go up in smoke. And he wasn't going to let that happen. Teddy Two Bears had his whole life ahead of him, disabled foot or not. And his family was barbecuing a buffalo for him.

And besides, Mariana Two Knives was nothing more than a wino. And winos were a dime a dozen, he tried to tell himself, but his heart felt like it had a rusty knife sticking in it.

He didn't know how to remove it. What's worse, he didn't know if he even wanted to. He stared as the eagles circled lower. They weren't eagles at all. They were turkey vultures, vile consumers of roadkill.

At War with the Snake People

Gus Winters raised his arms above his head and gave the sky both middle fingers. He was alone and he felt damn good. The pinto he was astride dropped several turds onto the ground and snorted. The spring morning was chilly and Gus was nearly finished riding the pasture, checking for newly dropped calves, when he heard an odd whirring sound. He felt the mare tense up beneath him.

"What the hell's that noise, girl?" he said and patted the horse on the shoulder. Gus craned his neck and tried to scope out where the strange sound was coming from. He couldn't see anything, but he thought the noise might be originating from the other side of a tall bluff covered with cheat grass and wild cherry bushes.

He led his mare up the small hillside and looked over the rise. Down in a small, washed-out gully, he spotted a jackrabbit. The rabbit was backed against a bank of clay by six rattlesnakes, their heads raised in an attack position. Gus was dumb-founded. He had never seen such a peculiar thing except one time he had smoked some crack cocaine, but this was real. It looked like the snakes had cornered the rabbit on purpose and were closing in for the kill.

Gus took a deep breath and scratched his head. Snakes weren't group hunters. Snakes didn't roam in packs—although his grandfather had told him a story about snakes that he'd never forgotten. In the late '60s, his grandfather had come upon a ball of snakes tangled together. He had been working on the new highway west of Martin, and he told Gus that a D-9 Cat had unearthed a snake nest in midwinter. They were rattlers and were all rolled together into a large ball about three feet tall.

Gus never knew whether his grandfather was pulling his leg or not because he ended the story by saying they'd poured gas over the snakes, cooked them up good, and eaten them. In fact, when he thought about it, he could never recall see-ing any snakes except one at a time. Now these snakes were in attack formation, acting weird, like something out of a sci-ence fiction movie. He didn't like the way it made him feel.

Things hadn't been going that well for Gus. Only the week before he'd gotten laid by a wino woman he'd hired to help his friend Teddy Two Bears lose his virginity. He'd gotten a little rough with the woman and popped her once in the left eye, blackening it. In and of itself, that little "love pat" was no big deal.

What was a big deal was that the woman, Mariana Two Knives, had been found dead the next day with a broken neck. Gus knew that neither he nor his buddies had killed her, but he still felt a deep sense of guilt and worry. He had talked it over with his friends who had been there that night and they'd agreed not to say a word to anyone. They had made a solemn vow of silence.

After they'd pulled a train on her later the night of the party, she'd gotten pissed and started throwing things. She'd smashed one of his parents' lamps. Luckily his parents and his sister had gone to Rapid City to stay overnight, but the next day his dad raised holy hell with him for partying at the house. His dad was hanging over and had been so mad that he backhanded Gus and knocked him down onto the living room carpet.

He was afraid of his father, and for good reason. His father had often beat the hell out of him. Once, when Gus had been drunk too, he had stood up to his father. His whiskey courage got him a visit to the PHS hospital emergency room. He learned his lesson.

Sitting on his horse, Gus rubbed his lip, which was still a little tender, and looked down at the incredible scene before him. He took a deep breath and untied his Remington bolt-action .22 from behind the saddle. He felt a sense of pity for the rabbit. The rabbit was bug-eyed and screaming a high-pitched squeal. Gus had never heard a rabbit scream before and it unnerved him. It sounded faintly human.

"Leave that friggin' rabbit alone, you knob gobblers," he yelled and released the safety on his rifle. "You don't wanna play fair, then okay, we won't play fair."

He took aim at the largest of the snakes and fired. *Blam!* The hollow-point .22 long rifle slug zapped the snake's head clean off its shoulders. Gus jacked another round into the chamber and fired again. Another snake fell over dead. A slow and delicious sense of exhilaration rose from his groin to his heart.

"Eat lead, you slimy bastards," Gus yelled. Deep down he envied the fact that his friend Teddy had seen combat in Desert Storm, even if he had lost his foot and had to wear weird shoes.

He aimed again, and when he did, he saw that two snakes had turned to face him. They seemed to focus their cold, evil eyes directly upon his own. Gus flinched and fired. He missed and gasped when he saw that those two snakes had broken off from their attack formation and were slithering rapidly toward him and his horse.

"Son of a bitch, what's going on?" he muttered.

The rabbit gave one more scream and fell over dead. It had tiny spots of blood all over its fur from the piercing snake fangs. Gus swore and fired twice more and killed two more snakes, but he had lost sight of the two that had taken off toward him. He wasn't about to wait for them to reach him. He grabbed the reins and wheeled his mare about. He kicked her in the flanks with both boots and galloped like a bat out of hell toward his house more than two miles away.

He put the horse in a corral near the house and took the reins, saddle, and saddle blanket to a small tack shed between the house and corral. He kept his .22 at his side. He broke off six inches of an alfalfa bale and tossed it to the horse and then walked toward the house. He took the rifle with him and scouted the ground thoroughly as he made his way to the front door.

His parents' car was gone and he assumed they were at the Long Branch Bar in Heinzville, Nebraska. It was Friday and usually on Fridays he and his sister, Theresa, had the house to themselves. He went to the refrigerator and took one of his father's beers. He drained it in less than a minute and let out a righteous burp.

"Quit being a pig," his sister yelled from the living room.

"Here's another kiss for you," he said and let out another earth-shattering beer burp.

"You're gross," she said.

"Gone partying, Mom and Dad?" he said to Theresa, who was sprawled out on the couch watching MTV.

"Now what do you think, Mr. Edison-Einstein?" she said, unimpressed with Gus and his attempt at coherent conversation. She was three years younger than Gus, a junior at the

Catholic high school, and she had plans to go to college. Theresa was a cheerleader, a straight-A student, good-looking, and had many friends. Her lot in life had been to become almost the exact opposite of Gus. He resented her success, but he secretly envied her. Why had she gotten all the luck?

"Whatcha watching?" Gus asked and squeezed onto the end of the couch near her bare feet. Theresa didn't answer him. He looked at her feet and then her long legs. She was wearing shorts and the angle of her legs allowed him a clear view of her white panties. A tiny tuft of black pubic hair crawled out from beneath them. He took a deep breath and pretended to watch the program, but every so often his eyes roamed and he glanced at his sister's private parts. Once he thought she had caught him in his act of secret peeking, but she said nothing.

Gus had never even fooled around at all with his sister, but occasionally he did have perverse thoughts about her. And once this past winter he had walked into her bedroom to find her naked atop her bed, fluffing her pubic hairs with a hairbrush. She had yelled at him and tossed the brush, which had narrowly missed his head.

He thought about that a lot and had even made that scenario an integral part of several masturbation fantasies. But, right at the last moment, just when the jizz geyser squirted, he would switch his thoughts, his vision, to another woman, any woman. That way, he figured, he hadn't even committed incest in his heart and God wouldn't punish him.

He sat blissfully, head moving from television to sister like he was at a tennis match. His sister was watching *Beavis and Butthead*. Gus didn't really understand them, but he watched anyway and pretended interest. He tried to make small talk with his sister, but she didn't want to be bothered.

"I never heard of no cartoon that sweared like them," he said and waited for Theresa's reply, which was slow in coming.

"The world's changing fast," she said, dismissing him.

"It is?" he asked.

"Not that you would notice," she giggled.

"Not that you would notice," he mimicked, hurt by the fact that she was always putting him down.

Sometimes he resented her know-it-all attitude. He sure as hell knew things she didn't. He thought about the gang bang and Mariana Two Knives and then evaporated the thought when he remembered that she was now dead. For an instant he debated whether or not to tell Theresa about the weird snakes he had seen earlier—.

No, he decided, that was too much like science fiction. His sister would giggle at him, or worse, think he had made the story up because he had nothing better to do. He simply shut his mouth and watched her and the television.

At eleven that night their parents called from Heinzville. Theresa took the call and a few minutes later told her brother the gist of the message. Their mom and dad were too far gone to make the drive back to the Rez through the pine-filled hills and were taking a motel room for the night if they could find one.

"Well, at least they called," Theresa said.

"Well, at least they called," he repeated, though this time he had made no conscious effort to mimic his sister.

"Give them credit for that," Theresa said.

"I do. I do. Most drunk parents on the Rez don't even do that," he agreed. He felt a slight twinge of guilt because he knew he was developing a drinking problem himself. He envied Teddy Two Bears because Teddy could take or leave the booze. It never really mattered to his friend. In fact, nothing much seemed to bother Teddy, although in recent days he had been acting very depressed and would not tell Gus what was bothering him.

"Yeah, I wouldn't talk too much about drinking if I were you," Theresa said, interrupting his thoughts. It was almost like she had read his mind. He blinked at her and she got up and went toward the kitchen.

"You'll probably end up just another drunken reservation Indian," she said as she sauntered out of the living room. She could be cold.

"We *are* Indians," Gus said, noting the strange sound of his words. Of course they were Indians . . .

Although they were *iyeska*, half-breeds, Gus was always puzzled by the sometimes anti-Indian streak that colored much of Theresa's thinking. He looked at her as she stood in the kitchen making herself a fried-egg sandwich. She was light-skinned like him, but she really could pass for a White woman. Maybe when she grew up, she would leave the Rez and become White. A lot of Indians did that. Fullbloods too. It didn't matter how dark your skin was. You could leave the Rez and become *wasicu*.

"Theresa, make me a sandwich too," he said.

"Dream on," she said and walked back to the living room where she switched channels and began to watch *60 Minutes*.

"I woulda made you one," he said.

"That was the last egg," she answered.

Gus shook his head and went to the kitchen. He made himself two peanut butter and mayonnaise sandwiches and took them to his bedroom. He took off all his clothes and stretched out on his bed, read a hot rod magazine, and ate the sandwiches. In twenty minutes, he was snoring out loud when a tremendous ear-shattering scream levitated him off the mattress. Then a second blaring screech. It was Theresa screaming bloody murder.

"Aiiiiiiiieeeeeekkkkk! Help!"

He jumped off the bed and ran out of his room. She shrieked again. She was in the living room standing atop the couch in front of the television.

"Theresa! What the hell's wrong?" Gus shouted at her.

"Snake, snake in here!" she squealed.

"Where? Where is it?" he demanded harshly.

"Over there," she said, pointing to a small bookcase. "It crawled underneath those shelves."

Gus ran to the corner of the room and grabbed his father's 12-gauge off the gun rack made of deer antlers. He jacked a shell into the chamber and gingerly crept toward the bookcase. He was shaking and too nervous to be bothered by his nakedness.

"There it is," she yelled, and Gus fired at a blur of motion on the floor.

"Got it," he said and let out a high-pitched giggle. "It's a damn garter snake. Hahhhh. Ain't even poisonous." He picked up the shredded serpent by its tail, waved it briefly at his sister, and then opened the front door and tossed it out into the night.

"Well, how should I know? I'm not a snake expert," she said.

"Damn, Theresa. It was just a garter snake. You didn't have to scream like that and scare the hell out of me. Sounded like someone was murdering you."

"Well, it scared the damn hell out of me," she said, still shaking, though her eyes were now focused upon a snake of a different nature. Gus had never heard her swear before.

"You're naked," she said.

"Well, you seen one, you seen 'em all," he said, making light of the fact that he was getting aroused.

"I've never seen one," Theresa said and nodded at his hardening penis with her chin. "Can I touch it? Please?"

"Jesus, Theresa."

"Please."

"I guess," he said, "if I can touch yours."

"Okay," she said. "But you gotta promise to never tell anybody. We shouldn't be doing this."

"I promise," he said and held his breath. His sister stood up and slowly removed her shorts and her panties. Gus stared hard for a moment and then reached to touch her. Her hand firmly grasped his penis as he gently stroked her, and in that breathless instant the front door burst open and their parents staggered in.

Gus spun around and faced his parents with a full erection. "He made me," Theresa shouted. "I didn't want to. He made me do it."

Theresa's brother's face turned crimson and he wished he were dead. And there was a damn good chance his father might just grant his wish. A damn good chance. His father's eyes were red, cold, and glassy like those of a deadly snake ready to strike.

The Pink Plastic Clothespin

Edwin Takes The Bow drank heavily for three months after he lost his job because Abner Red Eagle had been voted out of office. Then, one day, his wife finalized their impending divorce. Abner Red Eagle, his own cousin, had taken a job in Rapid City, and his own ex-wife was going to follow her boyfriend. She packed up and moved there. Edwin didn't really mind. He was due for a change.

Two months after his wife left, he sobered up one bright spring morning. He found a new job as a reporter for the *Eagle-Standard*, the reservation weekly newspaper. And he also found a new girlfriend, Delores Perreault, a half-breed woman who had been a second grade teacher for twenty years.

Delores was extremely fine-looking and was in her mid-forties. Edwin was thirty-six. The age difference mattered little. What was becoming a problem was that Delores drank too much and Edwin was now perched atop his home-built wagon.

That didn't stop them from shacking up together though. Delores was an exceptional cook and homemaker, and Edwin needed a home.

During dinner one night, Edwin happened to tell Delores that he was doing a story on a young woman who had just been murdered. When he told her that the name of the woman was Mariana Two Knives, Delores began to cry.

"You knew her?" Edwin asked.

"She was one of my students when I first started teaching," Delores sobbed and got up and mixed herself a vodka and tonic. "My first or second year teaching," she added and gulped down half of the glassful of fire water.

"Well, they found her with a broken neck down by the powwow grounds. Looks like she was murdered."

"Murdered? Who did it?"

"Don't know," he said. "Two hunters, you know Bobo Robidoux and Paulie Roan Horse? Well, they found her all covered up with branches at the powwow grounds. The tribal cops and the FBI are still investigating. I'm just now starting doing a story on her for the paper. Looks like she was beaten and raped before she was killed. She was just a wino."

"She was one student I'll never forget," Delores said sadly while she was mixing another drink.

"*Ennut*?" Edwin said. "Tell me about it."

"Oh, there's not much to tell."

"Tell me. I want to know."

A half hour later, under duress from Edwin and vodka, Delores began to tell her story.

"Oh, she was kind of like a little orphan girl. Insecure. Mad all the time," she said. "I really felt sorry for her."

"How old was she then?" Edwin asked.

"Oh, second grade, about eight years old. Very dependent on adult approval for everything she did. She had real dark skin and real shiny black hair. I don't know who her mother was, but her father was a bootlegger here on the Rez. She was a girl that was constantly craving attention."

"Why?" Edwin asked.

"Well, it was just the way she was. That was the way she was in the classroom."

"But why was she that way?" Edwin demanded.

"Who am I to judge why she was that way?" Delores pouted.

"But you were her teacher. Aren't you supposed to know why students are the way they are?"

"No, I don't know those kids when they first come in my room. You don't have a psychological profile of them. Some, like her, just hang around you all the time."

"It should take about five minutes to figure out where they're coming from," he said.

"No, you're wrong. Anyway, she was just constantly hanging around me, kind of getting on my nerves at times. From the very beginning. Like I was her substitute mother, but it was negative. She did things to get on my nerves like asking me dumb questions when I knew she wasn't dumb. If you asked her a question, then she'd rephrase it in a silly way. This happened years ago. It's not like I kept a diary about Mariana.

"She was just always hanging around me. Always had to be touching me, grabbing my hand in the classroom. And then being belligerent all the time. She was intellectually belligerent. Always confronting me and crying around like: 'You're always calling on him. How come you never call on me?' Most of the time I called on her, she knew the answers, but when I had playground duty she was always grabbing my arm and tattling on the other kids."

"I'm going to fix us a drink," Edwin said and got up. Delores didn't question his decision to start drinking again but simply continued her story when he returned to the living room.

"And then she was just kind of *onsika*, pitiful. Not poor, because she dressed in good clothes. I don't know who was taking care of her then, maybe her grandmother or her auntie Angie. She was well taken care of and never ate up all her food at lunch. She wasn't like some of those kids from really poor families who gobble their lunch like hungry wolves and then wait for someone who didn't like what was on their tray to offer it to them. Mariana was so demanding. She depleted me of my energy. I couldn't do enough for her. She was totally egotistical. Demanding."

"Well, she ain't making no demands now," Edwin chimed in.

"I felt compassion for her. I felt very, very sorry for her, but at other times, uh, well, I could have just slapped her face. At times I really didn't like her and had really repulsive feelings toward her. She kind of had me torn in two.

"I felt so sorry for her because I knew there was something that made her that way, and then on the other hand she would never relinquish the floor when I called on her and then she'd pout like: 'Poor little sad Mariana. You never call on me, but you always call on them. I know the answers too.' Then after a while I started feeling totally negative toward her. I just wanted nothing to do with her. I told myself I was a teacher, not a god damn social worker."

"So you rejected her?" Edwin asked.

"I just didn't want to bother with her. The hell with her. I'd refer her to a counselor or something. They'd investigate her home life or put her in a special class or put her in a home or something. They never did do that. I liked her. I was in conflict. I liked her and hated her. She was just always hanging around me. Mariana was really good when there were no other kids around. We'd just visit and chitchat and she'd tell me a lot of gossip about what was going on around the Rez. But in a group, she was a spoiler. If the kids would get enthusiastic about something, she wouldn't enjoy anything. She would just spoil their mood. Make some negative remark. Like flashcards. The kids would be doing really well, but she'd get upset when I'd praise them. She'd put them down. She couldn't take the competition. And her language, my God. She'd call them 'cunts' and 'assholes' and 'cocksuckers.' I don't know where she got that language.

"She was just very, very jealous of any other kid who had anything to do with me. Christ, when you have twenty-five kids, you have to pick the motivated ones to help you out. That's your support system. If the motivated kids back you, it makes teaching a lot easier. She never fit into that group. Mariana just wasn't motivated. Just wrapped up in her own little world. She had her own problems to deal with. She could have managed school easily, but she just did enough to get by. But she was bright. She carried one of those *Day by Day* books from AA. She'd sit there in class and read her book. Those AA books are written for adults, not for young kids.

"I don't know if she ever got any comfort out of it or not. It was a big, thick book. She'd get a little religious streak every so often, but she just couldn't function in everyday life."

"AA, huh?" Edwin said. "Speaking of which, hold on while I mix us another drink." When he returned, Delores continued.

"She did not like authority figures. You could not tell her what to do. You had to ask her if she would do things. It was so sad. Sometimes she'd be so tickled to do things for you. Almost ingratiating. She would do things for you that would make her look important and then sit back. Just sit there with her pen, looking very important. But nobody liked her. The kids didn't talk to her much. It's because of all the reasons . . ."

"Raisins?"

"Reasons, not raisins. I don't know. She was a little snitch too, a tattletale on the other kids. Just for attention. But she was so bright. She'd catch on to things so quick. She could figure things out. Later on, I found out her dad was a bootlegger. Well, I'm not making any judgments because my dad was a bootlegger too. But her dad killed a guy over some booze. Some guy came and tried to steal some whiskey, and her dad shot him in the head with a shotgun. Ended up in the state penitentiary."

"When was this? Who?"

"It was some White guy living with some local woman. About eighteen years ago, I guess."

"About the time I went away to college," Edwin said.

"I don't know if it was second-degree murder or what. Then she stayed with her aunt, and her auntie Angie didn't have much time for her at all. Angie was like married to AA, meetings, support groups, all that stuff. She unknowingly neglected Mariana. So that's the story."

"That's the story? What's the point?" he said in a loud voice and then laughed.

"There's no point. That's just her story. That year she was in my class was the same year my dad died. I remember that better. I took two weeks off when he died and then when I came back to school, she pouted at me for a whole week. Wouldn't talk to me at all. She thought I'd rejected her by being on bereavement leave those two weeks. She was silent in class that whole week. And then the following Monday, just as I was taking roll, she walked up to me in front of the whole class and pinned one of those little clothespins on my sweater."

"A clothespin?"

"Yeah, one of those little plastic toy clothespins. A pink one. She pinned it on me, smiled, and went back to her seat. She started talking to me again after that. But she was the same. Still demanding."

"That's it?" Edwin asked.

"That's about it," Delores said with tears in her eyes. "I lost track of Mariana for a while after she left my class. I guess about five or six years later, maybe when she was in the eighth grade, I heard she had started drinking and sleeping with boys. Then she fell in love with that Verdell Ten Bears. He was a couple years older. That was the last I heard."

"Damn," he said.

Delores got up and went to her bedroom. She returned in a few minutes and held her closed hand out to him. She opened it up and there was a pink plastic clothespin. Edwin bit his lip savagely to stop a large tear that was forming in one of his eyes.

"Well," he said. "I don't know if the cops will ever catch the guy who killed her, but someone will. You know how Skins are."

"You could tell way back then, even when she was a little girl, that one day she'd end up all messed up or dead at a young age. It was sad, but you could tell."

"Damn," Edwin sighed and walked into the kitchen and dumped his drink into the sink. "Us Indians are pitiful."

The Blood Thirst
of Verdell Ten Bears

In the beginning there's only a hint of dangerous things to come. My name is Verdell Ten Bears & I'm planning to kill me a man in Pine Ridge. How come us Indians are forever falling down the toilet to Hell? Why do I keep putting my middle-aged boy body in dangerous situations? I always ask "why," hoping that by poking my finger into the eye of pain, pain will be chickenshit & run & healing will come, but *ennut,* that never does happen. I go on stepping in the same pile of crap, winter after winter, woman after woman.

I'm not retarded & I'm not a slow learner. I'm forty-two years old & dashing through the gray stadium of South Dakota winter like a sex-crazed rabbit. I'm clutching her welfare check in my grubby, shaking paw & I've endorsed her name on it. I need the money & I'm doing a hobbling dash through sanded snow as fast as I can but I move like a retarded elephant with fire ants biting his balls. This is what happens when you drink hard twenty years. I crash through the cruddy clumps of snow to get to the Rapid City Bus Depot. Running is not my solution to the riddle of the universe. Each step is a "why." Each gasp pains lung air & no answer comes. I've got some money & I'm going back home to the Rez. Why? Why must I ask? For reals, I'm planning to kill me a man in Pine Ridge.

■ ■ ■

I dribble my lonely blubber towards the bus & think of my loony heart. Walk, wiggle, stop, shake, walk. I might look like a purse snatcher on the run but I ain't a crook. Stick a needle in my eye & damn hope to die. I used to be a pipeline welder. Laid a lot of pipe. I'm a Viet vet. Heck yes, I forged her check but Christ, we been living together for five years. The check was only for two hundred bucks & she'd just drink it up anyways. She must know I gotta return to the Rez. It was her who threw me out. Tossed me out like a used condom.

Her & her college ways. She even has a book on Moby Dick the whale. Jesus, I never knew nobody who had a book on Moby Dick. She made me try twice to read it but it was too hard & didn't make no sense. She said it related to us Indians but I don't see how. She thinks my brain is half-toasted & yet she claims to love me. She won't after she sees her missing check. So what? I went to the tribal community college for two years. She ain't the only educated one. At least I don't have a book on Moby. She never even liked the jokes I made on Moby's last name. Well, screw her & the whale she rode in on. I've gotta go kill me this dude.

■ ■ ■

I shimmer across the icewalk & just miss sliding into a Rapid City cop. She's a white whale, a bigfat Dickless Tracy. She gives me a fish-eye look & I look back at her gun & keep on shuffling down the road. She yells something at my back but I keep going. In the crisp air I have a vision of starving eagles.

Hah! This is a weird movie! In the corner of my eye, they flock. Dozens of the huge birds looping the loop. They are man-sized & have razor claws. They could rip a damn whale to shreds. One hushed swoop & the land could be ribboned with meat, puddled with blood. All for a lousy two hundred bucks I stole.

I'm getting paranoid. I imagine cars that follow me down the sidewalk, turning my footprints in the snow into a hundred faces of the man I'm going to kill. The face of death won't be so handsome. Death is a scraggly drag queen with smeared lipstick. How does a bullet feel? It slants silent in descent & then it rapes the flesh. I know. I been shot. But now I'm a little scared. Fat me, two hundred & twenty-six pounds, sweating, panting, my scrotum shriveling, my eyes stinging, I run like a morphadyke goofball to the bus depot. I'm carrying a stolen check & I'm going to buy me a gun.

■ ■ ■

Strange how everything goes without a hitch & I cash her welfare check. They take it with no questions at the Indian bar by the bus depot so I have a quick shot of Jack Daniel's & two bottles of Bud. I even buy a round for two *onsika* winos from Rosebud & get me a pint of Jack Daniel's to go. At the OK Pawn Shop I buy a .22 Llama pistol & a box of long rifle shells for sixty bucks. It's a cheap little gun for a cheap little life. Then, at Woolworth's I buy a package of three Fruit of the Looms. Don't want to be walking around in smelly shorts. I put it all in a big paper sack & walk to the waiting bus & climb in.

It takes off like a whining dog & looks like a fat silver whale. Smells like Lysol mixed with puke & pizza. Down inside the cave of the paper bag, the small pistol is shining black. It's the real damn thing. I try to close my eyes & sleep. The bus groans south towards the dead man who waits. A woman behind me is whispering in Indian to a small child with a pee-smell diaper. The kid lets out a storm of big screams. His mother clucks, his mother coos. The kid quits his crying & I start mine. My tears are inside the bottle inside the paper bag.

■ ■ ■

Bitter bile is snaking up my gut towards my voiceless throat. I'm getting seasick on this whale bus. I don't need Dramamine, but I wish I had the guts of guys like the astronauts. Those are the real heros of this silly country. They leave the home fires of earth & put their asses on the line. Who knows? There could be slime-dicked geeks up there in outer space whose only reason for living is to stick steel scalpel tongues into human brains. I've seen mutilated cattle in the Badlands, tits & ears cut off. There could be anything up there, even God, God forbid.

Astronauts got to got balls of brass. Or maybe they got no balls at all. I wish I had courage instead of pimples on the brain. The winter sun is dancing against the bus windows & everything. This old world is golden & pure. I wish I wasn't hanging over. This morning I took three Tylenol, a pot of black coffee, a hot & cold shower & a double shot of vodka. This shaking bus is going to make me puke & I'm sitting here thinking of asswipe astronauts.

■ ■ ■

I couldn't blame her if she called the cops on me though she never would. I wouldn't blame her for hating me. She's gotta watch out for her ownself & our kids first. I ain't had a steady job in years, but I'm grateful she's been supporting us for *dona* years on AFDC & welfare checks. She's good that way. I remember she was sitting on a bench in the park by the creek in Rapid City by the bronze Indian statue when I met her.

I was drinking "Green Lizard" & watching girls go by & she was looking good six years ago but now she's as big as me. I took her to the Oasis Bar & let her have her way with my ear for several beers & then we went back to the creek. In the bushes, not far from some winos sleeping it off, we did it in the dirt just like dogs. Now here I am carrying a paper bag

holding a .22 pistol. It's black & shiny & makes me feel ignorant. I smile when I get off the bus in Rushville & stroll towards the edge of the faded Nebraska town. I stick out my
thumb & the golden sun falls behind the pine hills. Twenty
cars pass me before some tuned-up Skins pick me up & swerve
me towards the South Dakota state line.

■ ■ ■

Riding in the fartsack Indian car to Pine Ridge Rez, I think of
her. Sometimes I used to feel like she'd completely blended
her mind with me like Spock's Vulcan mindmeld on *Star Trek*.
The *tahansis* in the car offer me some bad wine, which I taste
to be hospitable. Their sacramental bottle touches soon-to-
be-dead lips again & again.

*I think of how she made me get a cot in the basement of our
small house in Rapid. I quit sleeping with her. She knew I
didn't like fat women. Drunk once, she said if I had to pick up
some women, at least I'd have a place to bring them. Who are
you, my mother, I asked & then went out to a bar to see if I
really could. I couldn't & came home late to find her in bed,
cuddled up with a half-eaten pizza & a box of Whitman choco-
lates. Herds of beer cans surrounded the bed like all those little
candles in Catholic Church. I laid next to her & while she
snored, I did myself off.*

Two guys in the front seat are arguing & then the driver slams
on the brake & the two fools are out on the farmland highway
duking it out. I tighten my grip on the bag holding my gun.
Screw those guys, the driver says & peels out leaving their
swing-banging knuckles behind him. We pass through White
Clay & then hit Pine Ridge. He drops me at the Conoco station & I go in & get a cup of sixty-cent coff, bad-tasting coff.

■ ■ ■

Outside the Conoco, two boys are fist-fighting. How can a
man live a decent life? When I see white clouds dance past
the moon in the black night, I think of murder. When I see

black crows dancing on the fleshy rib cage of a road-killed deer, I think of snow. There is always the battle of lightness & darkness. This is the curse of my people. I could never put my nose to the grindstone. I stayed with my grandmother when I was growing up. She had a grindstone. We used it for sharpening knives & the axe. The axe was for killing chickens.

I found that if you catch a chicken & draw a line in the dirt in front of it, it will become paralyzed. If you draw an invisible line, the damn same thing will happen. Bend their head down & draw the line. They cannot move. Do this on an old tree stump & then you whack off their heads. But once their brain is gone, they wake up & do a wild, nasty-blood dance.

If you hypnotize two young cocks & make them face each other, they'll do a staredown for a long time & when they finally come to, they will fight. Just like the two boys outside are doing. Just like I am doing with myself, *ennut?*

■ ■ ■

Another time drunk I tiptoed into the house & peeked at her in our whale-sized bed. She was asleep crossways on the bed & it woulda took a D-9 Caterpillar to move her snoring flesh. I tried anyways. Every time I touched her, she moaned & spread her legs a little wider. All I wanted was some sleep, not nooky. She was half in the bag & was lying on a half-eaten Eskimo Pie, melted into a brown & white puddle under her huge melons. As usual, piles of Budweiser cans were scattered all around the bed. I went down to my cot in the basement & dreamed my usual dream. I think of that dream when I sit in Pine Ridge looking for the man I am going to shoot.

In the dream purple mountains in the distant horizon are crisscrossed with lines of gray smoke from woodstoves. Inside a small, once-whitewashed shack, a fullblood woman is pulling down a parched, cracked shade. She turns on a lamp & puts on a faded shawl. Then she takes a flashlight from a drawer & walks to the small outhouse behind the shack & cries in the dark.

I wake up sweating & I am sweating now when I think of that bastard I come here to kill. Mariana, you can't hear me, but this one's for you.

■ ■ ■

I think I see the buttwipe that I come down here to do in. He's just a kid. I leave the gas station & walk to my cousin Jake's house in the Crazy Horse Housing Projects. There I fit into the usual drunken dope party. It is getting dark outside & a light snow is falling.

They feed me but are disappointed when I refuse a hit of coke or a can of beer. I'm just tired, I tell them & they show me their dirty-sheet bed. While I'm sleeping an hour later, a man peeks into the bedroom & startles me up. He sure looks like the one I've come for, but he ain't. He's just another drunk Skin, bumbling through life, from hangover to picking beer cans.

I sleep & then wake again with the sweet mist of a forgotten sex dream & bad heartburn. It's four in the morning & the party is over so I walk through the living room, stepping over a dozen passed-out bodies & into the kitchen. I find some baking soda & mix a teaspoon with a glass of water. I burp & see the full moon of dull grade-school paper pasted against the kitchen window.

I find a full can of Coors someone has hidden & drink it slowly & think of nothing. I walk back into the living room & see a teenaged girl with a flat chest asleep on the floor. I lie down next to her & fall asleep with my lips pressed hard against her sweet, brown Indian face.

■ ■ ■

A hellish scream ricochets around the house & wakes the zombie drunks. It is the howling screech of a dog hit by a car. The night of the living dead drunks shuffle to the windows & check out the world. A quick-kicking German Shepherd is in the last stage of the spasms of death. It shrieks like a human wounded. Everyone looks for a weapon. One finds a bat, a woman finds a mop, the girl I sleep by grabs this broom. We go out to end the misery of the four-legged. Ten drunks beat & kick the dog under the fool's full moon until blood covers shoes & snow. It quits breathing.

I walk back in with the mumbling drunks & then gravity begs us to floor. The girl I've slept next to lies against me & silently undoes her blouse. In the dark stench of snoring & stinking drunks I touch her small breasts & say no words until I hear someone vomiting in a near corner. "Don't tell me your name & don't ask me mine," I tell her. She laughs a girl laugh & rustles my hair & says her name is Eileen. She's a sophomore in high school. I kiss her hand & then turn my back & I sleep hard for an hour or so until I dream of a bus bound for Hell.

■ ■ ■

Burping down the highway, the whale bus approaches the gates of Hell. A raspy voice grinds over the intercom: "Attention to all you hopeless Skins. Anyone planning to commit murder must exit at the next stop." I look in the bag & the gun smiles back. In the seat in front of me, a man with a bad face rash that oozes yellow fluid is passing out candy to children. "Tell him thanks," a dark mother warns her three children. The kids snicker & wink & the diseased man smiles timidly & walks like a spider down the aisle to the toilet at the rear of the bus. He leaves the door open & I watch him trying to scald the crud away from his reeking face with cold water. He paper towels his face & turns to face me & I see he's the one I'm going to kill but before I can move, the bus lurches into the Hell Bus Depot.

I exit the bus & wait on the platform, waiting to see this enemy of mine. But as the people come off the bus, they all have disfigured faces. They are all full of bullet holes & all have much saber slashes upon their dead bodies. They are all wearing ogle wanagi, the shirts of the Ghost Dance.

■ ■ ■

The Hell Bus Depot is the life of Indians living on this stolen land. We have government food: powdered milk & powdered eggs & tin-canned horsemeat stew & powdered potatoes & cardboard steaks stained with blood red grease. Inside, the survivors of the Wounded Knee Massacre are eating maggot-hopping food. Red eyes pervade. Straight razor carrying perverts from the state pen are prowling for action among the cavalry butchered dead.

In our station of the metro, tribal cops twirl bigdick batons & wear eagle feathers to cover their shame. In this dream mix of now & was I look in my bag to bring back the real. But in my bag are powdered whores, powdered winos & powdered Indian dogs. Outside a light powdered snow is falling & as I dance to the bathroom someone is singing "Jingle Bells." In the air of piss stench & cherry-flavored urinal deodorants, old men are scraping whiskers with wine bottle fragments. The egg-faced man is swabbing his face in fast-forward movements until it is varnished brown.

Awake, I can see clearly that this man, this damn enemy, is me & that is the lie this dream thinks it tells me.

■ ■ ■

We all have to go back with pain in our fat hearts to the place we grew up to grow out of. This is how we fully come to know ourselves I say to myself as I leave Jake Red Horse's house in the cold-ass morning. In the angry early-day sound of teens squealing tires on their way to high school, my Indian blood bubbles on the plains of my brain. I am living a lie.

For twenty years I been living a lie, sedated by alcohol, unredeemed by transfusions of flesh. I go one way. My life goes another. One foot forward, one foot backward, body lurching, arms flailing, wordless, wordless, this Indian dance. I light a cigarette & stand near a cedar & contemplate the fool's mission I'm on. Vietnam wasn't this crazy.

There might be more than one man here that I have ridden the bus down to kill. Maybe my plan was to do him & myself in & I'm not sure now that I will. Then again, the day is early. I scratch my head while the morning sun dances on snow-bundled children walking to school. Sometimes I'm a coward & life is ten pounds of shit in a five-pound bag. But sometimes I'm a stone-cold killer. Mariana, how come they killed you?

Waylon Two Stars
Takes His Son Rabbit Hunting

We had buffalo for food, and their hides for clothing and our tipis.
We preferred hunting to a life of idleness on reservations where we were driven
against our will. We preferred our own way of living.
We were no expense to the government then.
All we wanted was peace and to be left alone.

—Crazy Horse

Waylon Two Stars was born without Magi. His fifteen-year-old mother hobbled in slow, fearing pain four sacred times around and around the government-issue, whitewashed shack in Lakota winter until the chortling of crows eating a road-killed rabbit broke her water.

She went back in and to her amazement delivered the brown child herself. Giddy from pain, she named him Waylon and then she slept like the child she was.

■ ■ ■

At forty years of age, Waylon shimmied down winter's road halfheartedly avoiding turd birds, little brown fluffs of life that dive-bombed his car. In twenty minutes of fast sliding, he had killed a dozen with little guilt. Their deaths were almost comforting. Each small *whump* sounded like the cork-string popgun his mother had given him at seven when he'd

149

had the mumps. Microbes had traveled gland roads from jaw to groin, swelling his testicles like Christmas oranges given out by Our Lady of the Sioux Catholic Church ten miles from his house near Calico.

His mother, then twenty-two, had made little paper birds that she had tied with thread to a dangling light chain. Waylon shot and shot and with each hit forgot his hurting man-size balls.

■　■　■

Waylon's balls returned to normal (whatever normal is at the age of seven) thirteen days later, but the weight of manhood's early imposition then had cursed him for life, he thought, glancing at his own son, and driving from Porcupine to Wounded Knee through crazed flocks of brown-feathered *kamikazes*.

He tried not to think of the past, but the more he bit his tongue, the more unwanted images flew against his car and into his mind. A strategic retreat into the soft sanctity of childhood was often therapeutic, but when childhood came screaming for attention of its own, it was like a cage full of rabbits watching their brothers and sisters being butchered.

■　■　■

Waylon had known the taste of rabbits, wild and tame, and in the tune of his bounding youth had seen a mother eat her young after he had love-cuddled them. In his teens he had killed many rabbits his grandma raised for eating and he could not forget their ball-shriveling screams at the instant he put the axe to the soft fur of neck.

He had not eaten rabbit in twenty years, and the taste was nearly forgotten. He did recall his mother rolling the sliced flesh in flour. Something like chicken, he would tell any stranger sauntering through his mind. You fry them just like chicken. They go good at picnics and the last time he had eaten rabbit was at a picnic at White Clay Dam twenty years past on the week he was scheduled to depart South Dakota for the vacuum of Vietnam.

Dusty-faced Indian kids were running, carrying cantaloupe sliced into smiles, the juice forming tributaries of temporary sweetness down their chins toward their hearts. He sat on the tailgate of an old pickup talking to his girl, begging her to release the lock of thighs, but she never did and he cursed her throughout his tour of duty and never wrote back once after he shot his first man.

When he did return, he punished her by placing a ring upon her finger. And, in a few years, his wife graced his seed and gave him a son, but the next year she died drunk when Waylon rolled their car.

■ ■ ■

Waylon loved his son but felt uneasy staring into the large brown eyes of the ten-year-old boy. He couldn't quite figure out the feeling. It was something like being caught in a lie. Part of him was afraid that his son could see right through him, past viscera and bone into fear.

Looking at his son, Waylon saw his own lack of father and he saw the sins of his mother. He saw the shame of his race, its hopes and its nightmares. He saw himself and was happy, briefly, until he would think of the reason he was carrying cold steel. He was taking his son to hunt rabbits, and to stop the furry screaming inside his own skull, he reached over and mussed up his son's hair.

"What's rabbit taste like, Dad?" his smiling son asked, and Waylon shivered and laughed.

"Tastes like chicken." *Tastes like me,* Waylon thought and wished that his wife were still living.

Raven and the Valentine

Somehow, somewhere in the vortex of blackness, Raven saw a patch of shimmering black. This shimmering was his own iridescent wings flapping. Things were slowly beginning to lighten and he was not dead anymore. He beat his wings for all he was worth and flew toward a small speck of white light in the northern quadrant of the bleak blackness.

Then, it was like he was born again. He broke completely free of the darkness and found himself in the blue sky over a green land. Raven reached a horny claw up to his face and wiped away some beads of sweat. An invisible angel of relief fluttered in his heart.

"Grandfather, thank you," he cawed at the top of his lungs. "Thank you, thank you, *Aho*." He knew it had been the Great Spirit and not the White man's God who had revived him, who had made him reborn. It went without saying that given a second chance, he would be a good, very, very god damn good bird this time around.

"Oh, sweet beauty of life," he repeated to himself over and over for the next twenty minutes.

Several months passed and he took a job working as a teacher's aide at the tribal elementary school. It was a job that had its pros and cons, but it was a job, and he was determined to make the most of his new lot in life. He was helping to make life better on the Rez. "There could be no higher calling than working in the field of education" was the official party line.

On rough days when the kids were particularly dysfunctional, he always meditated upon the coffee mug the teacher he worked with had given him. It was white with a large red apple. On the back of the cup, in flowery script, it asked: WHAT ARE THE THREE BEST THINGS ABOUT BEING A TEACHER? And underneath those lines, it answered: JUNE, JULY, AND AUGUST!

It was Friday afternoon, and Raven was glad the week was ending. Because it was the first of the month and the welfare checks had come out, it had been a particularly disruptive week in the classroom. While on his afternoon break, he mused about how life had a strange habit of repeating itself. Although he was alive again, he had a sudden urge to start smoking again, so he jumped into the air and quickly flew to a nearby convenience store to buy a pack of smokes. Camels.

The line was long at the counter. There were several little Lakota girls giggling and talking in a hushed conspiracy. They had packages of valentines in their hands and were no doubt giggling over which boy should get a certain valentine. It was a nice scene—one that carried Raven back to his own childhood when he had participated in the ritual of giving valentines to classmates and secret loves.

He wondered if they still made those little heart-shaped candies with love messages on them. He thought of an Indian girl named Isabelle. Isabelle was the first human he had ever taken to a movie and she was the first girl, human or animal, that he had ever kissed. He daydreamed back to the tender moment his beak touched her lips. She had been the first girl to ever French-kiss him. Raven used to give her plenty of valentines when he was in elementary school.

But now, as he left the convenience store and headed back to the school and the teachers' lounge where he could consume nicotine, caffeine, and gossip, he felt a brief wave of vague depression. Once back at the school, he quickly dismissed all childish thoughts of things such as valentines. *Kid stuff and nothing more,* he decided and then felt uneasy with his adult thoughts.

Raven knew that Saint Valentine's Day, February 14th, was named in honor of Saint Valentine; but then, he never knew the guy and he had papers to correct. He hopped back to his classroom, still trying to put valentines out of his mind. They had provided a brief but pleasant reflection upon his past, his childhood. Back to work . . . so much for thoughts of the cute little cards and boxes of candy. And yet, one short minute later, the love, the sentimentality of Valentine's Day again exploded in his mind.

Raven knew the handwriting on the letter sitting on his desk. It was a strange combination of script and printing that he had seen many times in his past. The letter was from Isabelle. The girl he had gone with most of his high school days. His mind reeled momentarily. His heart slouched down onto his stomach and for an instant he felt like he had just downed several straight shots of Jack Daniel's.

My God, he thought. *Here I was just thinking of Isabelle and now a letter from her appears on my desk.* He had not seen her in over ten years and now this flashback from the past, this golden oldie ready for his mind's turntable. Raven was puzzled that Isabelle would even know where he now worked, and yes, he looked again—the letter had been sent to the school. He looked at the postmark. It had been mailed from the reservation. *So, so Isabelle's back in town,* he thought.

He opened the letter and before he could read it, a secretary in the principal's office called him over the intercom.

"Mr. Raven," she said, "please come down to the office. You have an *important* phone call."

"Did they say who it was?" he asked.

"I didn't ask them who they were," the secretary said in a tone that was not quite snotty, not quite matter-of-fact. He let her attitude slide and in fact would have a hard time ever holding anything against her because she had the finest backside he had ever seen on a human.

"Okay," he said and got up. Soon classes would be ending for the day and he'd have to help the teacher he worked with herd the monstrous children into the yellow buses.

"Isabelle's back in town," said the voice on the phone.

"Who is this?" Raven asked.

"It's Coyote, you nitwit. I just seen her and I thought I'd give you fair warning. I ran into her at Sioux Nation Shopping Center. She asked about you."

"She did?"

"That's what I just said—"

"She did?"

"Damn, yes, she did, Mr. Bird Brain. She wanted to know how you were doing. I said you were out working at the school, but she seemed to know that already. Then she said she already sent you a note."

"*Ennut?* She did?"

"Hey, man, you a broken record or what? Ain't you got nothing to say except 'she did'?"

"Don't know what else to say," Raven said.

"Yeah, well, I can't blame you. You should see her. A lard-ass living nightmare, man. Geez she's fat, fatter than Refrigerator Perry. And ugly too. Man, is she ugly. Looks like she fell from an ugly tree and hit every branch on the way down. Real rugged, kind of wino-looking. Scars on her face too. I'm telling you, cousin, the last time I seen a face that ugly it had a hook in its mouth."

"Hey, thanks for the report, Coyote. You're a real nice canine. I'm sure all the women libbers love you, but I gotta get back to work. See you after a while, crocodile."

"Well, us animal brothers gotta stick together. See you later, masturbator," Coyote said and hung up. Raven walked back to the classroom he was working in and picked up the letter. His claw was shaking like the begging hand of a dry-throat wino.

It was hard to read the scrawl, and Coyote's description of Isabelle kept popping into his mind. *The last time I seen a face that ugly it had a hook in its mouth.* He thought of the sweet, intelligent, and beautiful girl he had known and loved. He knew there would be no good news in the letter. No matter how good or happy she might sound, Coyote had just relayed her true situation over the phone. She was doing that old Indian trick of drinking herself to death.

"Isabelle," Raven whispered to himself and began to read the lined notebook paper in his claw.

It was a long letter. After her hello, how are you, and just thought I'd write routine, she began to speak with words that stabbed Raven like a dull, rusty knife:

I ran away from it all after I left high school. I ran from all the Indian-ness or mess and married a white man and went to live in the suburbs of Chicago. We never had any kids, so I went to college and got educated. I earned a B.A. in social work of all things. Well, eventually I broke up with my old man and moved into Chicago and began hanging around with other Indians. Well, you know how Indians get when they go to cities. I began to hit the juice heavy and started to drift from man to man.

Raven took a deep breath and blinked his eyes. Her words upon his brain tasted worse than the casserole recipe Coyote had learned from Old Bear and cooked for him once. He really didn't want to read any more of her letter. He wondered why she was telling him all this stuff. He lit a cigarette, forgetting that he was still in the classroom. Luckily, there were no students in the room. He began to read again.

You're probably wondering why I'm writing all this stuff to you. I don't know. I just had to get this off my chest and I remembered that you used to love me. Well, at least I loved you. Anyway, big cities have a way of chewing Indians up and spitting them out. We go to cities to get lost, or we go to die. Or most worst of all, some of us go to cities to become White.

You know how it was when we were growing up. How we had to heat our hot water on a woodstove and then fill a tin tub to take baths. How can we ever forget how we had to dig new holes for the outhouses, sometimes in the middle of winter when the ground was as hard as a rock. You remember how the White kids used to tease us because they had indoor toilets and we didn't? And we used to wear worn-out shoes and shabby, hand-me-down clothes to school? We lived hand-me-down lives. Our welfare existence was handed down to us. The Pope's version of Heaven was handed down to us. Everything was handed down to us. I wanted to get away from all that and I did, but now I'm back.

I guess I should never have left in the first place, but there wasn't anything to keep me here. Now, I think I've wasted a lot of my life. These days I'm still drinking and I guess I must look like hell. I'm sure I've got liver damage, and for what? Just to get away from the Rez and now I'm back here again. A little worse for wear, but damn, I'm glad to be home.

I guess I'll try to find some kind of job working for my

people, after I go on the wagon and clean up my act. But the main thing for now is that I'm home and that makes me happy. It really does! This is where I should be. In the cities I lived in, I saw so many Indians just totally wasting their lives—and why? I guess that most of them were just like me and wanted to escape from the sad little ostrich world of reservation Indians. I don't know, I'd like to get a job working with youth and help them stay off booze and stay on their own land. Lord knows I'm a bad role model right now. I've made my mistakes and it'll take me a little time to straighten out. Do you think you could write me a letter of recommendation or act as a reference? I'd really appreciate it. I still think of you, Raven. Happy Valentine's Day!

Raven took a deep breath and gently put down her letter. He looked up at the ceiling and thought of the sleek, firm body she'd had in high school. Her breasts were the size of softballs and—

"Teachers' aides report for bus duty," the secretary blared over the intercom. Raven hopped into the air and took a lazy flight to the parking lot, where the fleet of yellow vehicles were lining up.

As the noisy kids boarded their buses, he thought about the two giggling girls buying valentines at the convenience store. He wondered where they would be in thirty years. Would they be safe, sane, and surrounded by people who loved them? Would they try to remain living upon the land of their ancestors?

A million thoughts, both sad and loving, popped into his head during the remainder of his workday. And leading the parade of those million thoughts was one big one: *I'm going to write Isabelle the best fuckin' letter of recommendation that's ever been written in the long history of letters of fuckin' recommendation.* It would be Raven's valentine to a long-lost love. It would be Raven's valentine to himself.

Household Hints
for Rez Wino Bachelors

Edwin Takes The Bow was getting pretty sick of hearing all the same holier-than-thou drunks at the weekly AA meetings. He especially hated to hear Bobo Robidoux and Paulie Roan Horse, the two wino trappers. They hogged the whole meeting with their stupid sober stories of capturing mice or finding chicken eggs in their traps. Earlier in the week, he had written a paper that he would read to them. He hoped it would take the starch out of their shorts.

A secret smile formed in his mind later that night as he stood up amidst his fellow dried-out drunks and read his paper to the red-eyed coven:

Household Hints for Rez Wino Bachelors

1. When driving a nail into a piece of wood, blunt the end of the nail to keep the wood from splitting. Use only wooden

stakes for vampires. Use only sirloin steaks for good-looking women.

"Pshawww," Bobo interrupted. "That's a good one, Edwin, but who can afford steaks these days?" Edwin did not answer and in fact did not even acknowledge Bobo. He merely scratched his nose and continued reading his paper:

2. Never try to press a pair of pants by putting them between the box spring and the mattress. It will give you a backache for one, and two, you'll never remember where you lost your pants.

3. Never wear a white shirt while eating an Indian taco. Hawaiian floral shirts are recommended. These colorful shirts may also prompt local Indian women to start wearing grass hula skirts.

"In your dreams," Paulie cut in. "You show me an Indian woman in a hula skirt and I'll show you a twelve-inch whanger on Big Bobo here." The entire room of men burst out into guffaws, but Edwin continued. He was going to finish, come hell or high water.

4. When washing dishes with a bar of soap, always remember to put the soap back in the shower, or kill two birds with one bar of Ivory and take a shower with the dishes.

5. Never try to dry recently washed underwear over an open fire or in an oven. They will turn brown if they are not already. Dingy underwear can be soaked in bleach to make them look nice. Don't use too much bleach or you'll end up with holy skivvies.

"Ah, man," Paulie piped up, "that's the only way Bobo here knows which is the front and which is the back of his jockeys. The front is yellow and the back is brown." Again, the room burst into crazed laughter. Edwin even laughed too.

"Let me finish this damn thing. You guys talk all the time anyways. Show a little respect. When I got the floor then keep your traps zippered."

6. If you are a heavy smoker, you must remember never to empty ashtrays. At least once a month, usually on a Sunday morning, you'll wake up without cigarettes and an ashtray of half-smoked butts will prevent a nicotine fit. You drunks know what I'm talking about here.

7. If you find out your weekend snag is a second cousin or a closer relative, you must immediately say, "But you do know I'm adopted, don't you?"

"Edwin, I hear you're related to that Perreault woman you're shacking up with," some bleary-eyed coyote in the back chimed in. Edwin ignored him and continued. He knew he sure as hell was not related to Delores at all. The old coyote was just trying to demonstrate Indian humor.

8. Cook bacon, eggs, and potatoes in the same frying pan at the same time. This saves much time and work. It all gets mixed up anyway. And if you must fry bacon by itself, always add dish soap to the grease as you pour it down the sink. This will not only save a visit from the Roto-Rooter man, but will please any Sierra Club freaks in the vicinity. If you don't have indoor plumbing, don't worry about it.

9. If you have a lawn that needs mowing, wait until a strong wind is blowing away from your property. This saves raking. If you just have large weeds growing around your house, you can tell people, "That's how the Great Spirit intended it, and I'm a traditional guy."

10. When winos consistently come by and beg for money, tell them, "I'm sorry but I just spent my last two bucks on a bottle of Milk of Magnesia. And I just drank the whole bottle fifteen

minutes ago! Come on in and visit with me for a while."

11. If missionary Christians come to your door speaking of Jesus and won't leave, cross your eyes, pick your nose, and yell, "I'm a worshiper of whips, Voodoo, and vodka." If this doesn't work, try to borrow some money off them. Tell them you'll pay them back come Sunday.

12. Buy all your socks in one color. This way you'll never know if any are missing. If you're ever visiting relatives or maybe you're bored with your old lady and you gotta whack it, slip a sock over it first. Then when you spasm, the joy juice will be safely hidden inside a sock, no telltale Kleenex or stiff spots on sheets. Just make sure to let your sock dry before you put it back on.

"That's why it's so hard to hunt with Paulie," Bobo interjected. "We're walking through the woods and all I can hear is this *squish, squish, squish.* Do like he said, Paulie. Let your socks dry out first."

Not to be outdone, Paulie had to fire back. "The only *squish-squish* you hear is that melted Hershey bar on the bottom of your chocolate shorts. When you gonna learn that corncobs ain't the best way to wipe? Modern-day Indians use toilet paper or at least Sears and Roebuck catalogs."

Edwin rolled his eyes at the acoustic squares of the ceiling, took a deep breath, and read some more from his paper:

13. If you want to eat just one scrambled egg, shake it good while it's still in the shell. This will save you time. And you can use this same process for more than one egg. It saves on washing mixing bowls.

14. Women's hair spray can give your shoes a quick shine. It's also good for spraying moths, wasps, and spiders. It petrifies them solid.

15. If rattlesnakes are a problem around the house, get some chickens and let them run loose. Snakes will soon leave the area because they have a strong distaste for chicken language and chicken poop. Do not eat any chickens recently bitten by a rattler. If you ever see a large group of snakes together, bend over and kiss your butt good-bye because it's the end of the world. Remember the brother who had impure thoughts about the White Buffalo Calf Woman? Wasn't he devoured by snakes?

16. If you have a pair of cowboy boots you think are hopeless and are thinking of throwing away, try this salvage process. Put them in the washing machine with two cups of Clorox. Then when they're done, take them out and stuff them with paper towels to retain the original shape. Then take them out to your back yard and bury them.

17. If you are broke, unemployed, and constantly getting threatening letters from bill collectors, write back that you are currently in a mental institution for shooting a man who wrote you a similar letter seeking payment of a debt. Add that you still hear voices telling you to do it again and that it's probably a good idea if they don't bother you for a while.

"You got that right," Timmy John Pretty Bull spoke up from the back of the room. "That's about the first thing you said tonight that makes any sense."

"Jesus, I really appreciate your support, Timmy John," Edwin said and continued his interrupted reading:

18. It is not a good idea to get lost in the woods while hunting. When this happens, look on the north sides of trees for moss. Gather the moss until you have a pile twenty feet high. Then climb atop the pile and scream for help until someone comes.

"That's what Paulie does," Bobo screamed.

"No, that's what Bobo does," Paulie screamed back.

"Jesus, guys. I'm almost done. Just let me finish this damn thing and then I'll sit down," Edwin said in exasperation.

"Well, make it soon," an anonymous voice whined from the middle of the room.

"Almost done," Edwin said. "I'm almost done. At least you gotta admit this is better than Bobo and Paulie telling one of their horseshit hunting tales."

19. If you have a cat or dog that is shedding, borrow a vacuum cleaner and use it on the animal. This cuts down on a hairy house. If you want to get rid of the animals and you don't have the guts, put them out on the street on Mondays and Thursdays when that speed freak UPS guy blazes across the reservation. He's on amphetamines or something and has flattened more people and animals than you can shake a stick at.

20. Before you sell your used car, spray-paint the tires black. Wash the excess grease off the engine, buy a case of ice-cold beer, and then drive over to the prospective buyer's house with a carload of young, fine-looking women.

21. If none of the above hints help you in your bachelor-hood, get married. If your marriage doesn't work and your wife won't leave, start wearing her clothes. Tell her to go to work and you'll stay home and take care of the damn house.

22. If worse comes to worse, make some pumpkin moon-shine. Buy a ten-pound pumpkin. Cut it in half and take the seeds out. Fill the inside with brown sugar, put the pumpkin back together and bake for one hour at 350 degrees. Then throw the pumpkin away and go to bootleggers and buy yourself a fifth of whiskey. Whether you drink it or not is up to you.

Edwin now spoke off the cuff. "Whether you drink or not is up to you guys. If you do, then you'll have something original to say next week instead of the same old tired crap I'm always hearing from you, especially you two, Bobo and Paulie."

"You suck," Bobo yelled with the combined force of each one of his three hundred pounds.

"He's right about that," Paulie chimed in. The rest of the men were more generous, though. They stood up, wobbled slightly on their alcoholic legs, and politely applauded Edwin Takes The Bow.

Edwin bowed and beamed and wondered whether or not he would fall off the wagon later that night.

There Was a Coyote Woman

O Grandfather, creator of us all. Once there was a Coyote woman who howled at the lopsided moon and didn't know if she was human or animal. She thought she was skilled in dealing with men. She told her friends who were not really her friends that she had "lots of men—too many." This meant that she had a lot of dates.

"I got a date tonight," she would tell her cubs and then she would head out the door and be gone all night.

Well, they weren't really "dates." She just had lots of guys and these guys were not coyotes. They were human and humans from the bottom of the barrel. She had lots of guys in every way you could imagine. She had lots of guys who had no pride, though she thought that she had pride. To a man, her men had bad teeth and were high school dropouts.

In her canine heart, she knew that men just took advantage of her. "All you men want the same thing," she would tell them. The truth was that men took her for granted because she wanted to be taken for granted. They had no respect for her because she was always available. She was always in the bars even though she had three young coyote pups still in her den. She figured they were okay because they were teenagers and could fairly well take care of themselves. They had the TV to keep them in line.

But even her pups had no respect for her. They were in the Catholic high school and were starting to experiment with sex, booze, and drugs. The elder son had started dressing like an inner-city gangster. The daughter had let a priest fondle her three times in the past year. They never told her their problems. How could they? Their own mother was their main problem. And they never wanted to hear her problems.

"I love you kids," she would say to them, but they only gave her blank stares and remained silent.

"Who is that woman?" the three pups said to themselves one night shortly after their mother went out on a date.

"She's the one who'll be with some guy who enters our house tonight while we're sleeping," the elder son said.

Many times this coyote woman picked up men in bars and dragged them home to her den.

"Damn, we got another home horror movie tonight," her kids would whisper to each other after they were awakened by their mother's howling and panting.

"I'm a coyote and we got it rough," the coyote woman would tell her temporary lovers. Her men, mostly Indian guys, just shrugged and gave her the roughest versions of love imaginable. If she had no respect for herself, then she had no respect for womanhood, period, they thought. The truth was that these guys had no respect for womanhood in any measurable form. They saw her as a disgusting piece of fur who was only good in a pinch, only good in that dark desperation of closing time at the bars.

With a bruised soul, she sought punishment for being unable to understand and control her life. "Once us coyotes used to be free," she would say. And then she would utter her plaintive, never-ending question: "Why are you men all the same?" The men would shrug, smirk, and parade past her cubs on the way to her bedroom. Often they would wink at her daughter. Several had even winked at her sons.

"You want to be with me or not?" they would invariably say when she complained that they stared at her daughter.

"I'm with you, aren't I?" she would answer, but deep down she was puzzled and distressed by her constant state of heat. It was like she was addicted to sex, yet she got no real pleasure from it. She had heard that fat people had a gaping hole in their souls that they tried to fill with food. She knew what the hopelessly hefty were going through.

When the men saw how she treated her own children, and how she kept a filthy den, they usually left pronto. Sometimes they stayed and beat the hell out of her just for good measure. She thought this meant they cared at least a little about her. Why else would they waste their time and slap her around when they could be doing something else?

"I don't have to live by any rules," she would tell her coyote relatives. "Rules are for humans." And then she began to hang out with a motley crowd of drunks, a mixture of low-life humans and flea-ridden animals. In her group were the generic drunken Indians, a gay coyote cousin, a coke-snorting bear, a manic turtle who'd misplaced his shell, and other varied vagabonds with dyslexic souls.

"I got an advantage over my liver," she would tell her new friends when they congregated for liquid prayer services.

"Oh, here she goes again, trying to make a joke," her friends would moan and turn their heads.

"My liver ain't killed me so I ain't killed it! So, I guess you could say that I'm the liver—hahhhh," she would say night after night. And her friends would regurgitate fake laughter deep into the night, or at least until all the booze was gone.

O Grandfather, creator of us all. Once there was a coyote woman who howled at the lopsided moon and didn't know if she was human or animal. One day, quite by accident, she happened to meet an Indian man who cared. He cared about himself; he cared about her. He cared about his people and his land. If there had been any spotted owls on the Rez, he would have cared about them. He just plain cared.

"You men are all the same," she told him. "You just want one thing." The problem with her statement was that if a person asked her what that "one thing" was, she would always give an incorrect answer. She measured love in terms of sex. She did not understand love and probably never had. Worse than that, she could not love. Because she could not love, she could not be loved. But she did not understand this. She was rapidly approaching middle age, but more often than not, she thought with the mind of a teenage girl.

"Maybe I should get some counseling, but I sure ain't joining up with them AA's," she told her new beau, Elton Three Horses, in a rare unguarded moment.

"That's a good first step," he said, but she never took his advice. He was not the type to impose his will on her. Elton was a kind man.

Oh, sure, she knew that something in her mental makeup had gotten fouled up when she was in her teens. She'd had the urge then, as most teenage coyote girls do, to fall deeply, madly, and seriously in love with a handsome coyote man. But it had not happened.

She had lived with one coyote and he had fathered her pups, but he had always been roaming the countryside away from their den. And one day he got run over by a Pepsi truck barreling down the reservation's dirt roads. In occasional introspective moments, she would tell herself that she had loved him, even though she could barely remember his face or scent.

One time, years after he had been killed, she got extremely drunk and threw a brick through a friend's television when she saw Ray Charles singing his "It's the right one, baby, uh-huh" commercial about Pepsi-Cola. In an uncontrollable instant of coyote madness, she threw the brick, and then her friend threw her out of the house and never talked to her for three years. She was never really able to decipher why she had thrown that brick until it dawned on her that the father of her pups had been killed by a Pepsi delivery truck.

Time did not stand still. She often wondered why people went around saying that life got easier as you got older. She found it to be the exact opposite. Life got harder as you got older. And it was so damned hard, sometimes impossible, to break old, destructive patterns. Still, regardless of all the dark clouds in her life, it was a dream of deep and everlasting love that kept her going forward. There had to be one good man out there who would come in and not only sweep her off her feet, but make all her past mistakes disappear into the sunset.

O sweet, desperate coyote woman. She'd coddled and cradled her dream of finding a true love and it had never happened. Maybe, she thought, this was why she had run through the years from moment to moment. She had run from human to human, knowing that those experiences were hopeless, often dangerous, but doing so again and again and punishing herself in the process.

"Grandfather," she prayed almost every night, "oh, please, please, please, Grandfather, send me a good man."

And so it came to pass, and the man's name was Elton. He was that same Indian man she'd met who cared, and yet could not understand her. It didn't matter. He fell deeply in love with her. He was a good man, and not bad-looking. His full name was Elton Jerome Three Horses, Jr., and he was about the same age as her and, like her, had only a grass-roots education.

He was a hard worker who had spent more than thirty years working on various reservations for the Bureau of Indian Affairs. But then Elton retired early and, being a single man, returned to the reservation of his birth.

"Home is where your relatives are buried," he told her.

"Yes . . . it is . . . of course it is," she agreed, lightbulbs of epiphany exploding in her brain.

He had long ago learned to control his drinking, but the combination of being home for the first time in many years and then falling in love had started him drinking again. The twelve steps that he had followed out of the darkness now seemed to vanish like deer tracks in a rainstorm. Elton was home and in love and drinking like a fish.

Because this coyote woman was his age and because she reminded him of the reservation he had grown up on, he fell even deeper in love with her than he thought possible, so he had no choice but to help her straighten out. But all he did was start to drink heavier than he ever had because she frustrated him so much. The task seemed impossible. Sometimes he thought that she really didn't want to change at all. And he was no one to judge since he had resumed bottle-feeding himself too.

For a man who had spent his entire adult life roaming the American continent working for "the people" (although he really worked for the federal government), Elton was strangely unaware of the vagaries of coyote women. What he did know was that this woman represented the tragic aspects of the reservation in a nutshell. Her blood, sprung from his home soil, was also his blood. He was not ready to give up on her.

With her soft brown fur, firm body, and deep black eyes, she was not unattractive. In fact, her looks were a big part of her problem. Given a few drinks, she became even more attractive. But the booze was killing her. The slight yellow tint that colored her beautiful eyes gave strong hints of a soon-to-be rendezvous with the Great Spirit. And he decided he could not travel that dark road with her. Life was too precious.

"You keep drinking, you're gonna die and lose me in the process," he finally had to tell her.

"*Ennut,* you're right," she said. But she drank, and he stayed, and they were both miserable.

Oh, she had learned to talk Indian over the years, and when she did, she would tell Elton of the spirit world she had heard of long ago. She would talk Indian so good to him that he would think he had lost the spirit-blood of his own people. She talked better Indian than he did, and even this caused problems every so often.

"Don't you understand me?" she would ask again and again.

"Yes, I understand what you're saying," Elton would answer in Indian, and then add, "but I don't understand you."

"You understand me," she would howl at him.

"No, I don't," he would scream back at her.

"You men are all the same," she would growl.

Finally he had no choice. He stared deeply into her eyes and whispered, "If you don't quit drinking, then I'm going to kill you and hang your hide on my wall. Then I'm going to run off with your daughter."

"Go ahead, if you think you're man enough," she said and he slapped her face.

Their battle lasted for hours, weeks, and continued for two months. It took all their time and finally they got completely sick of it. They both surrendered. They awoke one morning amidst the wreckage of their house and decided to join up with the AA troopers. Eventually, they both learned the twelve-step tango. They stopped drinking and decided to get married since they were in the house face to face all the time anyway.

O Grandfather, creator of us all. Once there was a coyote woman who howled at the lopsided moon and didn't know if she was human or animal. Finally, she came to see that she was a coyote and then she became skilled in dealing with one man.

She finally fell deeply in love with one man, an Indian man. She gave a prayer of thanks because she knew that man would become a wonderful stepfather to her pups. Well, he would at least give it his best shot. And she knew she would become the good mother they had missed for a good portion of their lives. She would freely repay all the love that she had long withheld from her own children. At least, that's what she told herself. It was only a white lie.

"Life ain't so bad," she told her husband on the day of their wedding. "Sometimes you just gotta sit in the dark for *dona* years, not just waiting for the movie to begin, but waiting for the good part to come on."

"Of course, you're right, my sweet, sweet love," Elton said as he drove his new used car away from the courthouse and down the highway to their new life.

About a mile from the courthouse, they had a head-on collision with a speeding UPS truck. They both had to be removed with the "jaws of life," but both lived, both lived happily (most of the time) ever after, the man, his wife, and her kids.

And every time they happened to discuss their accident, they would cry, then pray, and then kiss and kiss and then make soft and wonderful love. And when they made soft and wonderful love, they would both cry large tears of gladness. Jumbo tears. Holy reservation tears.

Old Bear Dreams
of the Comet of Despair

Old Bear awoke from his winter cave and stumbled out into the spring sunshine. He was hungry and his fur was all ratted. He'd had horrible dreams all through his hibernation. Apocalyptic dreams, dreams of dead bear relatives mounted in museums. And he had re-dreamed the dream of Great Bear, his grandfather. That dream was filled with screams and thousands of brick smokestacks rising starward, filling the sky with the black, bilious smoke from human flesh. Great Bear had called that particular dream he'd had in 1939 "The Dream of the Comet of Despair."

Great Bear had been a tremendous dreamer and was famous for years because most of his dreams came true. But he was even more famous because he had a tremendously huge whanger, and he used it often, and with relish, on human women. But his main fame came from "The Dream of the Comet of Despair." That dream had been recorded on all the winter counts of the animal kingdom. It had come true shortly after the Nazis began their rape of those lily-livered nations that included Czechoslovakia, Poland, the Balkans, and the Baltic States.

Old Bear envied his grandfather. He envied him for the dream of smokestacks belching human fleshsmoke. Adolph Hitler had made that dream of crematoriums come true, and for a while the animal world was abuzz with the glory of wondrous possibilities. *Maybe all the humans would destroy themselves in this new world war . . . Maybe these assholes would wipe themselves out!*

But that had not happened. Life on Mother Earth's back had actually gotten worse for the animal nations. Despite all the gun-toting two-leggeds killed in flesh factories and on the bloody battlefields of World War II, the human race had prospered and increased. Great Bear used to tell his grandson that the two-leggeds were "worse than rabbits."

"You put two of them out in the forest, the next thing you know there's a city with two newspapers there and thousands of yahoos going off to college on the GI Bill," his grandfather said one day. "One of these days there won't be none of us left. Stick close to the Indians. They're our only hope."

And Old Bear had forever envied his grandfather for the lucky stroke of his massive manhood, too. Old Bear's own endowment left a lot to be desired. He was only an average-sized bear. And he didn't even like sexing humans that much, although like most of the animals on the Indian reservation, he had sampled their bland fare on occasion. Nevertheless, throughout his whole life, he had wished for a larger penis. But at the very top of his wish list was the wish to dream a dream as powerful as "The Dream of the Comet of Despair." And now he had done so.

Old Bear stretched his massive frame and yawned. He went strolling, hoping to find someone to talk to or something to eat. "The Dream of the Comet of Despair" still spun in his brain. His dream had been the exact same as his grandfather's dream. He really *had* seen the tall smokestacks belching black human fleshsmoke toward the stars. But America was not at war now. What could it mean?

Old Bear put the dream out of his mind and sauntered into the small Rez village. It was not quite noon and most of the townspeople were still sleeping it off. He went to the Taco John's and ordered sixteen tacos, no lettuce, and lots of extra-spicy sauce through the intercom. Then he walked to the window and paid the cashier with a bagful of nickels and pennies. The cashier frowned when she had to count the change.

"Whatcha do, mug some little kid's piggy bank?" she asked and then snapped her eyes at him.

Old Bear did not reply. He simply leaned his large bear head through the window and brought his nose next to hers. Then he let out a large breath and she staggered momentarily and then regained her composure. Old Bear's winter breath was as rank as rank could be. She was wide-eyed and didn't say a word when she handed him his large bag of tacos and taco sauce.

Old Bear decided to walk out to the old powwow grounds and eat his lunch quietly under the warm spring sun. In ten minutes he reached his destination and began to inhale the tacos. He drizzled each one with two packets of the extra-spicy sauce. Fireworks exploded in his mouth and throat and then his stomach. Damn, they were good, he thought, but not as good as the big pot of beans and ham hocks he would cook tonight.

Old Bear bagged up the wrappers and dropped them into a rusty trash barrel. Then he walked into the grove of cottonwoods to relieve himself. As he was doing so, he happened to look up and what he saw made him pee all over his leg.

"Holy Christ, what you doing up there?" he yelped at the young boy suspended from a branch of the tree.

"Hey, can you hear me?" Old Bear said as he shook his penis. "Can't a bear even get some privacy here?"

The boy said nothing. Old Bear squinted and looked closer. The boy was hanging from the branch by a short rope tied around his neck. The stupid boy had done himself in. Old Bear's stomach began to turn sour. He took a deep breath, climbed up the tree, and cut the rope with one hand and held the boy with the other. He gently slid down the tree and placed the boy upon the ground.

"I never heard of an animal committing suicide," he said to the blue-faced boy. "How come you humans are into that? Life's never that bad that you gotta waste yourself."

Old Bear looked around the spring growth and spotted some new sage blossoming. He grabbed a clump and after some effort, managed to light it with his Bic lighter. Then he prayed. He prayed to his bear ancestors. He prayed to the four directions. He prayed to the Great Spirit. He prayed to Great Bear. He even prayed to Jesus.

"All that is holy, bring this boy back to life," he chanted.

"All that is holy, bring this boy back to life," he screamed.

And it happened. In less than three minutes, the boy came to, grabbing at his throat, gagging and kicking.

"Take it easy," Old Bear said and kneeled before the boy. "Take it easy, son. You're alive now. You're alive now."

"How?" rasped the boy. "I thought—"

"Don't think, just rest," Old Bear told him. "There's a water faucet somewheres around here. Just stay calm. I'll get you some nice cool water to ease your parched throat."

"Thanks," the boy said when Old Bear returned with his cupped paws full of water a few minutes later. "That's good."

"What's your name?" Old Bear asked the boy.

"Teddy Two Bears," the boy answered.

"Two Bears. Hmmmm. Good name. How come you went and stretched your neck. Suicide's a bad thing to do. It's more of a question than an answer."

Teddy told him the whole sordid story of his homosexuality, how Mariana Two Knives had died, and how he had heard on the Moccasin Telegraph that a man named Verdell Ten Bears was looking to kill him.

"Ten Bears? What is all this Bear naming crap with you Indians, anyways? Us bears don't go around naming our kids Jimmy Nine Indians, Johnny Seven Sioux, Jennifer Eight Apaches."

"Hey, I don't know. All I know is I heard that guy was gonna kill me, so I thought I'd take the easy way out. I had too much pressure on me. Either way, it would break my mom's heart. Either way, if that guy killed me or I hung myself dead." Teddy stood up and stretched his legs and tried to walk. His limp was more pronounced than ever.

"What's the matter with your leg?"

"I got wounded in Desert Storm. A land mine."

"You look too young to be a veteran."

"I am. I was over there."

"And here you're a vet, you been in the army, and still you want to do yourself in? You gotta get your head on straight, kid. Life ain't that bad, boy. The way you tell it, it wasn't your fault really that woman jumped from your car. Her time was up. That's all."

"She wouldn't be dead if it wasn't for me," Teddy said.

"And you wouldn't be alive if it wasn't for me," Old Bear said and put his arm around the young man. "Come on home with me. You can stay there until this thing blows over or at least until that Ten Bears guy comes to his senses. I got a big bed."

"Well, I don't know," Teddy said. "I never been with a bear . . ."

"For Christ's sake, kid, I ain't asking for your hand in marriage. I just want to take care of you for a while. It's up to you."

"Well, I'll go with you and we'll see what happens," Teddy said.

"Yeah, sure, we'll just see what happens. Come on. I want to get home and get some beans to soaking. We'll have us a good dinner tonight. I just can't figure why I had that dream though."

"Dream? What dream?" Teddy asked.

"I dreamed my grandfather's dream. The one about black smoke from human flesh rising up and darkening the sky."

"I've seen that," Teddy said.

"Pshawww, what on earth are you talking about?"

"Yeah, I saw that over in the Gulf. When those Iraqis set all those oil fields on fire, dark smoke towered up and blacked out the sky. I been back almost six months now and a lot of those fires are still going."

"Nawww, really?"

"Yeah, your dream sounds exactly like what I saw over there."

"Well," Old Bear said and scratched his rear. "Maybe that explains why I had that dream. It was an omen. It was a message that I would find you and save your life. Yeah, that makes sense. I probably never really had my grandfather's dream at all. I just got a death transmission from you. *Ohan,* now it really all starts to make sense."

"Maybe," said Teddy.

"Oh, yes, of course it does," said Old Bear. "One thing, Theodore," he added. "No more of this dying crap. You want to stay with me, you gotta promise that you won't go back to no hanging tree. No more thoughts of suicide. Promise?"

"I promise."

"And one other thing," Old Bear said. "I sure hope you like beans. Tonight I'm gonna make the best beans you ever had."

Teddy burst out laughing and ran back toward town. He had a change of mind and decided he'd take his chances with Ten Bears rather than Old Bear. He'd find him and tell him the truth. Maybe he'd listen. Maybe he wouldn't. On the Rez, life was a daily gamble. Sometimes God squished you like a bug. Sometimes you sucker-punched God. Sometimes!

Closing Song:
"Coyote's Circle"

I.

In South Dakota and heading west
Coyote was hurtling down the highway
and wishing for a drink, watching
a fly trapped inside the air-conditioned tomb
smash its head again and again against
the invisible God of the windshield
so he stopped the car
and chased it from front to back
with his cigarette lighter
until the concept wearied him
and he wasted it with his fist.

II.

Northern Nevada. July and he's zipping down
the desert interstate between Lovelock
and Winnemucca when a spew
of foam in the corner of his eye
shoots ten feet into the air
and Coyote's got the only car around
so he slams on the brakes and shakes
his head to make sure he's not
having an acid flashback and prays
that the oddball geyser on the barren
and baked land will not be a precursor
to alien spaceship landings.
He slowly backs the car up the hot tar
until he comes to the spot where
white foam shot high into the sky.
He gets out with pistol in hand and sees three
cans of Coors on the scorched sand.
One has exploded and the other
two are due any second.
Coyote releases the safety and fires, freeing
warm spirits born to be ice cold.

III.

Near Provo Utah the squeaky-clean
hardass State Storm Trooper
who pulls Coyote over for speeding
also fines him for not wearing
his seat belt and glares at his
dentures on the front seat.
He tells Coyote to remove the eagle
feather dangling from his rearview